Dead Wolf

(Kiera Hudson Series Two)
Book 6

Tim O'Rourke

ISBN: 9781090935892

Story Editor
Lynda O'Rourke
Book cover designed by:
Tom O'Rourke
Copyright: Tom O'Rourke 2012
Edited by:
Carolyn M. Pinard

For Patrick & Richard

Don't leave the station without me...

More books by Tim O'Rourke

Kiera Hudson Series One

Vampire Shift (Kiera Hudson Series 1) Book 1

Vampire Wake (Kiera Hudson Series 1) Book 2

Vampire Hunt (Kiera Hudson Series 1) Book 3

Vampire Breed (Kiera Hudson Series 1) Book 4

Wolf House (Kiera Hudson Series 1) Book 5

Vampire Hollows (Kiera Hudson Series 1) Book 6

Kiera Hudson Series Two

Dead Flesh (Kiera Hudson Series 2) Book 1

Dead Night (Kiera Hudson Series 2) Book 2

Dead Angels (Kiera Hudson Series 2) Book 3

Dead Statues (Kiera Hudson Series 2) Book 4

Dead Seth (Kiera Hudson Series 2) Book 5

Dead Wolf (Kiera Hudson Series 2) Book 6

Dead Water (Kiera Hudson Series 2) Book 7

Dead Push (Kiera Hudson Series 2) Book 8

Dead Lost (Kiera Hudson Series 2) Book 9

Dead End (Kiera Hudson Series 2) Book 10

Kiera Hudson Series Three

The Creeping Men (Kiera Hudson Series Three) Book 1

The Lethal Infected (Kiera Hudson Series Three) Book 2

The Adoring Artist (Kiera Hudson Series Three) Book 3

The Secret Identity (Kiera Hudson Series Three) Book 4

The White Wolf (Kiera Hudson Series Three) Book 5

The Origins of Cara (Kiera Hudson Series Three) Book 6

The Final Push (Kiera Hudson Series Three) Book 7

The Underground Switch (Kiera Hudson Series Three) Book 8

The Last Elder (Kiera Hudson Series Three) Book 9

Kiera Hudson Series Four

The Girl Who Travelled Backward (Book 1)

The Man Who Loved Sone (Book 2)
Kiera Hudson & the Six Clicks
The Six Clicks (Book 1)
The Kiera Hudson Prequels
The Kiera Hudson Prequels (Book One)

The Kiera Hudson Prequels (Book Two)
Kiera Hudson & Sammy Carter
Vampire Twin (*Pushed* Trilogy) Book 1

Vampire Chronicle (*Pushed* Trilogy) Book 2
The Alternate World of Kiera Hudson
Wolf Shift (Book One)

After Dark (Book Two)
The Beautiful Immortals
The Beautiful Immortals (Book One)

The Beautiful Immortals (Book Two)

The Beautiful Immortals (Book Three)

The Beautiful Immortals (Book Four)

The Beautiful Immortals (Book Five)

The Beautiful Immortals (Book Six)
The Laura Pepper Trilogy
Vampires of Fogmin Moor (Book One)

Vampires of Fogmin Moor (Book Two)

Vampires of Fogmin Moor (Book Three)
The Mirror Realm (The Lacey Swift Series)
The Mirror Realm (Book One)

The Mirror Realm (Book Two)

The Mirror Realm (Book Three)

The Mirror Realm (Book Four)
Moon Trilogy
Moonlight (Moon Trilogy) Book 1

Moonbeam (Moon Trilogy) Book 2

Moonshine (Moon Trilogy) Book 3
The Clockwork Immortals

Stranger (Part One)
Stranger (Part Two)
Stranger (Part Three)

The Jack Seth Novellas

Hollow Pit (Book One)

Black Hill Farm (Books 1 & 2)

Black Hill Farm (Book 1)
Black Hill Farm: Andy's Diary (Book 2)

Sidney Hart Novels

Witch (A Sidney Hart Novel) Book 1
Yellow (A Sidney Hart Novel) Book 2

The Tessa Dark Trilogy

Stilts (Book 1)
Zip (Book 2)

The Mechanic

The Mechanic

The Dark Side of Nightfall Trilogy

The Dark Side of Nightfall (Book One)
The Dark Side of Nightfall (Book Two)
The Dark Side of Nightfall (Book Three)

Samantha Carter Series

Vampire Seeker (Book One)
Vampire Flappers (Book Two)
Vampire Watchmen (Book Three)

The Charley Shepard Series

Saving the Dead (Book One)

Unscathed

Written by Tim O'Rourke & C.J. Pinard

You can contact Tim O'Rourke at

www.facebook.com/timorourkeauthor/ or by email at
kierahudson91@aol.com

Author's Note

This book was going to be called *'Dead Water'*. *'Dead Water'* was going to be split between both Kiera's and Murphy's POV. Just like Isidor in 'Dead Angels' and Jack in 'Dead Seth', Murphy has an important back story, which is woven into the series. While writing 'Dead Water' it became clear I wouldn't be able to tell Murphy's story in just a few chapters like I had originally believed. Murphy's story has turned out to be a novel in its own right with lots of twists, turns and action. Like Isidor's and Jack's , Murphy's story is important to the overall series and he holds important clues and links to what has gone before in Kiera's world and what is still to come. Therefore, I didn't want to cut the story back as we find out why Murphy deceived Jack Seth as a boy, why he was so opposed to Kathy Seth's and his brother Peter's secret relationship, and more importantly how he came by his slippers!! We also find out what happened to Potter and whether he makes peace with Kiera. So, instead of mixing the two books, I've published this book, *'Dead Wolf'* *Kiera Hudson Series Two (Book 5)* first and will publish *'Dead Water' Kiera Hudson Series Two (Book 6)* early next year.

Take care

Tim

Chapter One

Kiera

It wasn't true! I refused to believe that Jack Seth was my brother. How could I be related to him in any way shape or *form?* I knew who my mother was. She was the police officer who went to the Ragged Cove to investigate the disappearances of those people who had once lived there. She had that kind smile, pretty eyes, and just like me, she had jet-black hair. She had been the one who had whispered in my ear, 'See you later, alligator' as I had set off for school each day as a girl. My mother had been hooked on the red stuff by Phillips and Rom – she had in turn been seduced and betrayed by Luke – Elias Munn. Jessica Hudson had been a Vampyrus – not a wolf. She had been my mother and I refused to believe anything different.

"You lie!" I hissed into Jack's face.

The windows rattled in their wooden frames, like old teeth in loose gums. Jack looked back at me, a cruel smile pulling the corners of his mouth up into the shape of a crescent moon. "You know I speak the truth," he said, fixing me with his crazy stare.

I slapped his face with the flat of my hand, the sound of it like a gunshot in the dim light of the room. Jack's head rocked to the left. A thin line of blood trickled from his right nostril and onto his upper lip. The urge to lean in close and lick that blood away was unbearable. He saw me watching the blood, and he slowly licked it away with the tip of his tongue.

"I hate you," I spat, leaning away from him.

"Hate?" he smiled. "A feeling so passionate it borders on love. Don't you think?" The chains which fastened him to the chair clinked together in the darkness. "Don't you love your brother?"

"You're not my brother," I breathed, shaking my head.

"You know it's true," he said, this time his smile faded. "Look into my eyes, Kiera, and you will see for yourself. See how your father betrayed me and you. Watch your friend, Murphy snatch you as a baby from the dead waters and..."

Stop it! I screamed at him, screwing my hands into fists by my sides.

"You can't look because you know what I say is true!" he suddenly roared back, leaning forward in the chair I had chained him to. "We are brother and sister – you know it! I think we've always known it. I felt a connection between us the day I first saw you, and you felt it, too. At first I thought it was just lust – but it was more than that – it went deeper than that. It wasn't lust – it was love that I felt for you."

"That's why you killed me?" I spat at him. "That's why you..."

"Oh, please," Jack hissed back at me. "Don't flatter yourself. I never so much as touched your skinny little butt. When you threw yourself at me in The Hollows, I looked into your eyes and I *was* overcome with lust; that is true. But not for you – but for the simple act of killing. Yeah, I ripped your throat open, tore your liver and heart out, but I never did anything else – there was something which stopped me. At the time I didn't know what. Only when I came here to this house and saw you in the photographs with Father Peter, that I truly began to understand the connection I had – *we* had – for one another."

"So why have you had me believing that you..." I started in disbelief.

14

"Would it have mattered what I'd said?" he shot back. "You had me all figured out, didn't you? The vicious rapist and killer. That's how you've had me tagged from the start. Why bother telling you any different? Besides, I wanted you to hate me as much as I hated you for betraying me in The Hollows."

"Do you still hate me?" I asked him.

"More than you will ever know," he said, his eyes fixed on mine.

"But why, if it's true that we are brother and sister?"

"Because you had what I always wanted," he spat, unable to take his eyes from mine. "I just wanted a family. Father Peter took my dad from me, then left me for you. For years he treated me like a son, but as soon as you came along, he left. He chose you over me."

"None of this – this hate you have for me – is because of what happened in The Hollows," I breathed. "You hate me because you believe I stole the man you loved as a father from you. You believe if I hadn't have been born, you and Father Peter would have carried on pretending to be father and son."

"He chose you over me!" Seth barked. "While you were growing up, blissfully unaware of what your father was really like, while you sat on his knee and he told you stories, I was left to raise Nik as my son, to find him food, shelter – to survive. Not once did he think about that. Not once did he think of me. I was just a boy when Father Peter and his brother, Murphy played that cruel trick on me. Do you have any idea how I felt when I saw Father Peter's coffin taken beneath ground? I spent my life believing he had taken his own life because of the misery my mother – *I* had caused him. When all the while, he was playing happy families with you and the woman you believed was your mother."

"She *was* my mother," I barked back at him.

"Kathy Seth was your mother," he shot back. "She was my mother, too."

A thick silence fell between us like a heavy set of curtains. I could hear the snow pelting against the windowpane behind me, and the wind howling around the eaves. I looked at Jack tied to the chair and desperately fought the nagging feelings of doubt which now tried to consume me.

"You didn't turn evil because of anything Father Peter – my father – did," I whispered. "You didn't let the curse consume you because I was born, you didn't know about me at the time. You chose to turn bad because you were weak."

"*Weak?*" he roared. "I let the curse take me because I had to survive. You have no idea what it was like for me trying to survive each day. You were the lucky one. You grew up in the nice house with mummy and *daddy*. What chance did I have?"

"You didn't have a chance, Jack," I shot back. "You had a *choice*. There is a difference."

"It's easy for you to say," Jack sneered back at me. "Little miss goody-two-shoes. You've never known suffering. Perhaps if you'd gone through what I've been through. You've had it so goddamn easy."

"*Easy?*" I cried. "You call this easy! I lost my mother and father only to discover that I'm some kinda freaking half-breed from the underworld. I've got wings, claws, and a set of teeth a rabid dog would be proud of. In the last year, I've been chased, imprisoned, beaten, attacked, and hooked on the red stuff. Not only have I been murdered, I've seen all of my friends murdered, only for all of us to come back from the dead to this fucked up world that has been *pushed*. I'm being stalked by a bunch of creepy statues, berserkers, Skin-walkers, and any other hideous creature you might want to add. Not only that, I have the added bonus of turning to stone unless I drink blood, my lover is a no good, lying cheat, and I've just discovered that I have a long-lost brother who is a freaking serial killer. And to top it off – the cherry on the cake – I've just discovered that I'm part-freaking-werewolf! So don't you dare tell me that I haven't had my fair share of pain and hurt. I've had enough to last me two lifetimes."

"Okay, so you've had a few difficulties, too," Seth said. "But don't you see? That just makes us the same."

"I'm nothing like you," I shot at him.

"We'll see," he half-smiled at me.

"And what's that s'posed to mean?" I demanded.

"Your *choice*," he said.

"I'm not making any choice," I told him.

"It looks like you've already chosen me over your father," he said, his eyes shining like two pale yellow discs.

"What are you talking about?"

"Instead of finding your father some help for his wounds," Jack smiled, "you chose to chat shit with me, while he bled to death..."

Wheeling round and remembering my father, I raced across the bare floorboards towards him. How could I have forgotten that he was lying bleeding on the floor? I glanced up at Jack to see his eyes shining back at me from the darkness. One of them slowly closed as he winked slyly back at me. He had tricked me. Jack had sucked me into the conversation – taking my mind from the room and my dying father. He had caught me with his stare.

I placed my hand against my father's face, and his skin felt cold and stiff, like taut cloth. His eyes were open, as was his mouth. A pool of sticky, black blood covered the front of his shorts, where it had pumped from the openings Jack had made in him. I lifted my father's lifeless body into my arms, and the gap in his belly opened like a huge, grinning mouth. Twice now in my life I had cradled my father in my arms as he lay dead. The first had been in a white, sterile hospital room, this second time, in a room with bare walls and no carpets, and a serial killer laughing at me from the shadows in the corner.

Chapter Two

Murphy

The snow drove horizontally across the windscreen in thick flurries. The wipers fought to keep the screen clear. Violent gusts of wind crashed into the side of the police van, and I bit down on the end of my pipe as I tried to steer around the narrow, winding roads. It was dark now, and the two thin cones of light shining from the headlamps reflected back off the falling snow, making each flake glisten like glitter.

"I thought you said we were going to the Fountain of Souls?" Kayla shouted over the howl of the wind.

She was right, I had said that. I had lied, though.

"And we are, but not just yet," I said, glancing in the rear-view mirror at her.

"Where are we going then, if not to the Fountain of Souls?" Sam asked, sitting next to Kayla in the back of the police van as it lurched from side to side over the uneven roads. "Isn't Potter going to meet us there with Kiera?"

I had lied to Potter, too. Not because I'd wanted to deceive him in any way, but I knew there was every chance that he might be intercepted by those Skin-walkers. Potter had shown little resistance in the past to their mind trickery. My intention was to go to Kiera's father's house and hold back – just in case. Half of me had wanted to go with Potter, for us all to go together, but making peace with Kiera was something I knew Potter had to do alone. That didn't mean I couldn't be close by, though, to help save his arrogant butt if he needed me to.

I slowed the police van, changed gear, and guided the van around a tight bend in the road. With my pipe dangling from the corner of my mouth, I spoke around it and said, "I told Potter that we were heading for the Fountain. There is every chance he might run into some of those wolves." Then glancing in the rear-view mirror again, I glanced at Sam and said, "No offence, kid, but those wolves are not to be trusted. They've pulled that mind-bending shit on Potter before. He falls for it time and time again. He's either as thick as fuck, or he has a secret hard-on for them. But should Potter come across any of the wolves, and they trick him into telling them where we are heading, then he will tell them the Fountain of Souls."

"So where are we really heading?" Kayla asked, peering at me via the rear-view mirror.

"Kiera's father's house," I grunted, keeping one eye on the road.

"But I thought Potter wanted some time on his own with her?" she said back.

"What Potter wants and what he gets are often two very different things," I said, blowing pipe smoke from the corner of my mouth. "We're just going to hold back, should they be walking into a trap."

"Do you think they are?" Sam asked.

I didn't answer him straight away. I thought of Jack Seth, Kiera's father, Kiera...

"Perhaps?" was all I eventually said in response to Sam's question. I couldn't be sure of anything anymore.

Then, in the distance, something blue and white reflected back in the headlights of the van. I switched them off and slowed the vehicle to a crawl. The thick, black tyres crunched over the carpet of snow which covered the road and the rocky stone walls on either side of it.

"What's up?" Kayla whispered, getting up and leaning over the front seats so she could stare through the windscreen. "What have you seen?"

"Over there," I said, pointing into the field that stretched away on the right-hand side of the vehicle.

Sam appeared beside Kayla, and both of them screwed up their faces as they tried to see through the wall of falling snow outside. "I see it," Sam whispered, his breath hot against the side of my face.

"See what?" Kayla breathed.

"There's another police van in that field. There are wolves, too," Sam explained, sniffing the air, and I couldn't help but be reminded of Isidor.

"What else can you..." Kayla started.

"Shhh!" Sam silenced her with a wave of his hand. "Open the window."

I slowly wound down the window, and immediately leaned backwards as a gust of freezing cold wind blew a flurry of snow into my lap. Sam leaned over my shoulder, and thrusting his nose through the opening, he sniffed at the air. "Potter," he whispered. "I smell Potter."

"How can you be so sure?" I asked, not really doubting him, but hoping that perhaps he was wrong. Potter should have reached Kiera's father's house by now.

"Nicotine," Sam whispered, his eyes closed as he twitched his nose left and right.

"That's just my pipe you can smell," I said, blowing smoke over him.

"It's different," Sam said, his eyes still closed. "The two smells are completely different."

"But..." I started.

"Wait!" Kayla cut in. "Sam is right. I can hear Potter...he is crying out in pain...he's hurting..."

I didn't need to hear any more, and shoving Sam out of the way, I pushed the van door open and sprung out into the cold snow. Within seconds, both Kayla and Sam were beside me. Then, in the distance, I could hear the faint sound of wolves howling excitedly. Over this, I heard something else – the sound of someone crying out in agony.

Potter!

I glanced at Kayla, her bright red hair looking pink beneath the shower of snow that already covered her head and shoulders. "Ready?" I whispered, taking my pipe from my mouth and tossing it onto the driver's seat of the van.

"Oh, I'm so ready," she smiled back at me, her claws springing from the tips of her fingers like a set of ivory knives.

I turned to Sam to find him already crouched on all fours, his face looking more like a wolf than a boy. Thick, snow-covered dreadlocks swung from his head, the sides of his face, and beneath his chin. A long snout protruded from the front of his face, and his eyes shone a fierce, fiery yellow. A pink, fleshy tongue lolled over a set of vicious-looking teeth.

"Ready?" he barked at me, his hind quarters, which were now covered in thick, brown fur, flexing with muscle as he readied himself to spring over the slate stone wall surrounding the field.

"Ready," I nodded at him grimly, slashing my police shirt to ribbons with my claws.

"Murphy, you've ruined your shirt," Kayla breathed.

"Fuck my shirt," I barked, as it fell away in strips.

With my ribcage feeling as if it were breaking apart inside of me, I released my wings from my back and shot into the air. I looked left to see Kayla racing alongside me. Even though her face was a mask of anger and hate, she still looked innocent and beautiful somehow. I looked down to see Sam bounding across the field below. Great plumes of snow

22

showered up from beneath his mighty paws. I looked ahead, and seeing the police van, I arrowed my wings out behind me and raced towards it. The cold air threw my silver coloured hair back off my brow, and I could feel the skin which covered my face rippling with the pressure at the speed I was now traveling. The world seemed deathly quiet as I focused in on the scene below me. I could see what looked like a heap of rags surrounded by a pack of Skin-walkers. Each of them was dressed in a police uniform, as they kicked, punched, and clawed at the pile of old rags. But I knew it wasn't a pile of old clothing that they were ripping to pieces; it was my friend, Potter.

I fought the overwhelming urge to scream out in rage, but all good coppers know that you approach silently or the criminals scatter – flee the scene of the crime. That way you only get to fuck with one or two of them – I wanted to fuck with all of them. Arching my back, I spun through the air like a missile. I glanced right to see Kayla shooting through the air, her arms tucked into her sides to give her greater speed and propulsion. Both of us, as if in some way in tune with each other, dropped silently out of the black night sky, and skimmed just inches over the bed of snow which covered the field. Sam raced alongside me to my left. His dark brown fur was flecked with snow, and his tail stuck out behind him, as stiff as an arrow. Then facing front, I shot my arms out and snatched two of the unsuspecting Skin-walkers up into the air with my claws. Before they'd had the chance to even gasp in shock and surprise, I had smashed my forehead into the face of one of them, spreading his nose across his face like a rotten tomato. I drove the claws of my other hand into the throat of the second Skin-walker, the feeling of his neck breaking in my fist filling me with grim delight. Turning back to the first, I lunged at his face with my fangs. A giant flap of skin came away in my mouth and I spat it out. Even in the darkness, I could see the Skin-walker's tongue jerking behind the hole I had created in the side of his face.

"Thought you would fuck with my friend, did ya?" I roared, tearing back his scalp with my fangs before the Skin-walker had a chance to answer. With his body falling limp in my grip, I tossed the corpse away and set about the second Skin-walker. His head lolled to one side like a ragdoll. Its eyes spun in their sockets as the creature made a dying attempt to change into a wolf. Tightening my grip around its throat, I gripped the top of its skull with my free hand and yanked. There was a brief tearing sound, as the Skin-walker's head separated from the rest of its body, and my chest and face suddenly turned hot as a jet of black blood splashed over it.

Holding the Skin-walker's head in my fist by its hair, I back flipped through the air and raced down towards the police van and where Potter lay on the ground. It was then, in the distance, that I saw what looked like a row of statues spread out across the field. Each of them was looking up into the sky, their arms raised as if in prayer. I looked away, and using the Skin-walker's head like a cannon ball, I shot it through the air at one of the Skin-walkers who was still attacking Potter. The decapitated head smacked into the face of the unsuspecting Skin-walker and I heard a sickening thud. He fell backwards onto his arse. I looked at Potter. He lay face down in the snow. It wasn't white, but red, black, and sticky-looking.

The Skin-walker who was on his arse leapt into the air, and in a flash of fur and razor-sharp teeth, he had changed into a giant wolf. He spun around in the snow, howling up at me, its giant tail swishing angrily to and fro. I circled above it and was just about to drop from the sky, when Sam pounced from the darkness and launched himself at the wolf. Sam almost seemed to straddle it, as they both collapsed in the snow, rolling over and over in a mass of fur and claws.

I needed to get to Potter, who still lay lifeless in the snow as three other wolves continued to attack him. Dropping like a stone through the night, I raced towards him, my wings flapping on either side of me in the screaming wind. Then there were only two wolves, as Kayla appeared like a blaze of red lightning, punching one of her claws through the back of one of the wolves. Her fingers shot out of its chest, black with blood and holding the creature's heart in her fist. With her free claw, she ran her fingers over the throat of the second wolf. There was a fine spray of blood and it threw up its hands with a look of surprise on its face. Then as if its head was attached to its neck by a hinge, it toppled backwards, coming to rest between its shoulder blades. Kayla kicked out with her foot, knocking the decapitated wolf over. It toppled into the snow where it lay headless, twitching and jerking. At the same time, she withdrew her other claw from the chest of the first wolf. Just like the other, it had this ridiculous look of surprise on its face. Kayla had attacked so quickly, it was like the wolf was trying to understand why this winged girl was hovering all around him, with his still-beating heart in her hand. As if to prove to the wolf that he wasn't seeing things, Kayla bit into the heart she held as if it were a juicy, red apple. Blood sprayed over the face of the wolf. It made a gargling sound in the back of its throat and fell down onto its knees. As if to help it, Kayla stamped on the wolf's head, driving its face into the snow.

"That was for my brother, Isidor," she said around a mouthful of heart.

I looked away and spied the last Skin-walker driving its boot into the back of Potter's head, and lunged out of the sky. Eating hearts wasn't my style, but taking heads off was. With my claws sticking out before me, I took the head off the Skin-walker as easily as if slicing through jelly. Its head spun away. Even before I'd heard it thump into the snow, I was crouched down beside Potter and lifting him up.

"Potter!" I barked, and could see that his face was swollen black with bruises and blood. I had never seen anyone take such a beating before. His head lolled to one side in the crook of my elbow. "Potter!"

Nothing.

I glanced up to see Kayla had joined in the fight with Sam and the last Skin-walker, who had changed into a wolf. The creature was howling in pain as Kayla and Sam set about it with their fangs and claws. Kayla looked as if she was enjoying herself. Sensing that they would both be all right, I turned back to Potter.

"Come on, Potter!" I barked. "Look at me."

Nothing.

I shook him in my arms.

"You'd better open your eyes, or I'm going to rip you a new arsehole myself," I roared down at him.

"I didn't know you felt like that for me," Potter suddenly croaked just above a whisper, his eyes closed.

To hear him speak, however juvenile his remark was, made me just want to grip him tight in my arms. Then, looking down at him, I dropped him back into the snow and barked, "Quit laying around in the snow and act your age."

Potter groaned in pain as he hit the ground. "You took your fucking time."

"Shut your mouth," I snapped at him. "If it hadn't of been for me following your sorry arse, you'd be dead by now."

"He doesn't want me dead," Potter said, coughing up a wad of blood and spitting it into the snow. "He's trying to frame me for the murder of some wolf kid and teacher."

"Wolf kid and teacher?" I said, looking down at him as he tried to claw himself to his knees. "I leave you alone for five freaking minutes and you go and kill a school kid and his teacher."

"They were wolves," Potter cried out in pain, gripping his ribs with both hands. "Besides, one of them tried to seduce me..."

"Seduce you!" I shouted in disbelief. "Don't tell me you..."

"Nearly..." Potter cut in as he took short, shallow breaths.

"What does nearly mean?" I snapped at him. "You were meant to be coming out here to make up with Kiera for getting it on with Susan..."

"Sophie..." Potter wheezed.

"Whatever!" I snapped at him. "I'm glad you can remember all of their freaking names, because I can't, there has been so many. What is Kiera gonna say?"

"I thought it was Kiera," Potter breathed, holding out his hand for me to help him stand. "Help me get up. I'm bleeding."

"Quit your moaning. You've got a few cuts and grazes. You'll live," I told him, ignoring the hand which he held out towards me. "Besides, when did Kiera become a school teacher?"

"The wolf-bitch..." Potter started, falling back onto his knees. "She did that fucking wolf mind-trick on me. She made me believe that I was with Kiera."

"Jesus, Potter! Don't you ever learn? If one of these fucking wolves tried to sell you magic beans, you'd buy them!" I shouted at him. "In the future, will you do us all a big favour?"

"What's that," Potter winced, still holding his sides.

"If one of these wolves ever tries to sell you a talking parrot, check to see that there isn't a tape recorder stuffed up its freaking arse!" I snapped, walking away, leaving him looking sorry for himself in the snow. It was then I noticed that Kayla and Sam were nowhere to be seen.

"Kayla!" I called out. "Sam!"

No answer, just the sound of the wind blowing across the field.

I crunched through the snow to where I had last seen Kayla and Sam fighting with the wolf. The ground was covered in blood, but whose? I wondered. I spun around, the snow swirling all about me in the air. I looked for tracks, but there were so many leading to and away from where the fight had taken place. I cupped my hands around my eyes and looked in all directions across the field. The snow continued to fall so thick and fast, that visibility was now only just a few feet in all directions.

"*Kayla!*" I roared at the top of my voice. "*Sam!*"

Only the howling wind answered me.

With my eyes almost shut tight against the snow, I peered again into the distance. I couldn't see them anywhere. Even the statues I thought I had seen earlier had now gone.

Chapter Three

Kiera

With tears rolling silently onto my cheeks, I lay my father gently onto the floor. I slowly closed his eyes with the flat of my hands. In my head, I kept trying to tell myself that the man on the floor wasn't my father, not the one who had raised me as a child in the other world – the one which hadn't been *pushed*. If I kept telling myself that, then the pain I now felt inside wouldn't feel as sharp and cutting. Maybe I could reduce it to a dull throb. I turned away so I didn't have to look upon his face. I couldn't. I didn't want to. Had my father really been the man who had treated Jack like a son for most of his childhood? Had he been the man who had deceived Jack and left him all alone to fend for himself and his brother, Nik? More importantly, had my father really been the man who had mixed with a Lycanthrope and was I the result of that mixing? If it were true, then both Jack and I had been deceived by my father. I couldn't hate him, though, not like Jack hated him. But didn't he have reason to? If what Jack had said was true, then my father had murdered Joshua Seth to keep my birth a secret.

Then, still kneeling beside my father's corpse, I looked up at Jack and said, "Who else knows about me? Who else knows what I am and where I came from?"

"The people who are still living, you mean?" Jack smiled back at me.

"Yes," I nodded.

"Just me and your friend, Murphy," Jack said over the sound of the wind blowing hard outside in the dark.

"Do the Elders know?" I asked, wondering if that was the true reason I was being punished. After all, I was the result of a forbidden act, carried out by a Lycanthrope and Vampyrus. Wouldn't they hate me – despise me? Didn't I go against all of their natural laws, just like the half-breeds? But weren't the relationship between Vampyrus and humans forbidden, too? Hadn't those relationships been outlawed by the Elders because none of the children lived past the age of sixteen? Didn't that make Murphy a hypocrite? He had refused to help and support Father Peter, my father, because of his relationship with Kathy Seth, but he had mixed with a human and had two daughters. They had both been half-breeds, murdered at Hallowed Manor by Sparky and Luke.

Jack sat quietly and watched me from the shadows. "Do the Elders know about me?" I asked again.

"I don't know," he said with a casual shrug.

"Did they know that Murphy had mixed with a human and had two half-breed daughters?" I said, standing up and wiping the tears from my cheeks.

"You catch on fast, sister," Jack grinned.

"What do you mean?" I asked, moving across the room towards him.

"You already see the double standards set by your friends," he said. "Murphy wouldn't help our mother because her relationship was forbidden by the Elders. Or perhaps it was more because he just didn't approve."

"What do you mean, Murphy didn't approve?" I asked, standing before Jack, and looking down at him.

"Maybe if Murphy's brother, your father, had been mixing it up with a human, then he would have helped," Jack said, looking up at me. "But our mother wasn't human, she was a wolf and we all know how much Murphy and your other friends hate the wolves. They treat us like some inferior species to them. It's like we are not fit to be their equal. It's only now that I know the true reason why I hated that holding house. We were kept there like animals, waiting for the Vampyrus to find us homes. They weren't finding us homes; they were spreading our numbers, diluting us. In such small numbers, we were no threat to them. We were weak. Only together are the Lycanthrope strong. Who put the Vampyrus in charge? Who gave your friend, Murphy the right to police us? What makes the Vampyrus more superior to me or you?"

"But you're a murderous race," I said back, wondering if Jack were not speaking some truth or just screwing with my mind again.

"The Vampyrus have done their fair share of bloodletting throughout history," Jack sneered. "It wasn't the Lycanthrope who was running around feeding off humans and turning them into vampires. It wasn't a Lycanthrope who was trying to kill off all of humankind so he could have the Earth as his own – it was Elias Munn – a Vampyrus. They are in no position to dictate to us how we live our lives."

"There is no *us*," I insisted. "I'm not like you."

"It makes no difference what you believe," Jack said with a casual shrug. "I haven't lied to you, Kiera. There is a part of you that is very much like me. Whether you like it or not, you are half Lycanthrope."

"Even if what you say is true, I will never be like you," I hissed. "I refuse to be. You say I have a choice, Jack. Well, I make my choice. I choose the Vampyrus side of me – not the wolf."

"We'll see," Jack smiled straight back at me. "We'll see."

"See what?" I snapped at him, fighting the urge to wipe that knowing grin from his face.

"When Potter arrives, which he will," Jack said. "We'll see who you choose."

Chapter Four

Murphy

"Where have they gone?" Potter groaned in pain, staggering to his feet.

"If I knew that, do you think I would be standing in the middle a fucking snow blizzard calling out their names?" I barked at him. I wasn't mad at Potter, not really, I was mad at myself. Although I was pissed at him for going and getting himself in the shit again with the wolves. He attracted the wolves like flies around shit.

I looked at Potter as he lurched through the falling snow towards me. "How did you get here?" he wheezed, his hands pressed against his ribs and blood running from the cuts on his face.

"The police van," I said, checking the horizon again for any signs of Kayla and Sam.

"Perhaps they've gone back to it to take shelter," he suggested.

"I doubt it," I said. "They would have stayed here."

"It's a shame Kiera isn't here," Potter said, looking down at the crisscross pattern of foot and paw prints in the snow.

"How's that?" I asked him.

"She'd only have to take one look at these tracks and she'd be crawling around on her hands and knees, telling us how many there were, how tall, their weight, what they had for freaking breakfast, and the last time they blew their nose," he half-smiled as he thought of her.

"Well you want to thank your lucky stars she ain't here," I grumbled.

"Why?" Potter said, looking back at me.

"Because she'd kick your freaking arse, that's why, numb nuts!" I barked at him. "It's not like she wasn't pissed at you already, and now you've gone and humped a school teacher. Christ knows what she sees in you."

"I didn't hump her," Potter groaned, spitting a clot of blood into the snow. "And she wasn't a school teacher..."

Not interested in his excuses, I cut him dead and said, "You say Jack Seth is behind all of this? How can you be so sure?"

"As one of those Skin-walkers was kicking me in the bollocks, I heard him mention that Jack Seth wanted me alive," Potter explained.

"Then we're in a whole heap of shit," I said.

"What's new?" Potter said, snapping his broken and swollen fingers back into place.

"Do you have to do that?" I glared at him. "It sounds fucking disgusting."

Potter looked at me and opened and closed his fists, the sound of his finger joints popping and cracking sending gooseflesh up my back. "I can see you're starting to feel better."

"I ain't gonna feel right for another couple of hours or so," he said, arming away the blood that dripped from what looked like a broken nose. "I think they've broken every single one of my ribs."

"We don't have a couple of hours to spare," I told him. "If what you say is true, then I'm guessing that Seth got to Kiera's father's house before her and..." I paused, fearing what might have happened to Kiera – what she might have learnt – if Jack and her father...

"And what?" Potter snapped, fishing around in his trouser pockets and pulling out a crushed packet of cigarettes. He took one from the packet, which was bent over like a limp dick. He straightened it out, popped it between his lips, and then lit it. He drew deeply on the cigarette, then coughed, the sound of his broken ribs rattling like a bag of bones beneath his chest.

"You want to think about quitting," I told him.

"And what?" Potter asked again, the flat of his free hand pressed against his ribs.

"And we don't know where Kayla and Sam have disappeared to," I said, pushing the thoughts of what might or might not have happened with Kiera and Seth from my mind. For now, at least. "We can't leave without them, but we don't have time to go searching for them, either; not if we're to go and save Kiera."

"Let's start back at the van," Potter winced, setting off across the field, a trail of thin, blue smoke ebbing away from the cigarette which dangled from the corner of his bloody mouth. I followed, taking one last look back into the snow, hoping that I might see Kayla and Sam somewhere.

There was no sign of any track marks back at the van. In fact, the snow was coming down so hard and fast, it had covered any sign of the footprints we would have made earlier when leaving the van to save Potter. I snatched my pipe from the front seat and lit it.

"Well?" Potter asked me.

"Well, what?" I snapped at him, not knowing if we should go to Kiera or search for Kayla and Sam.

"Don't you see I was right?" Potter said, yanking open the back doors of the police van and reaching inside.

"Right about what?" I grunted, taking one of the long, black trench coats Potter had taken from the van. I put it on, covering my wings, and pulling the collar up about my throat.

"Teen-wolf," Potter said, flicking the butt of his cigarette away with his thumb and forefinger. "Sam has taken Kayla. He waited for you to turn your back, and then he snatched her. They're probably halfway to the Fountain of Souls by now."

"He didn't take her," I snapped at him, deep inside hoping that Potter was wrong.

"When are you going to stop putting your trust in these wolves, Sarge," Potter wheezed, his chest rattling again. "They do nothing but lie and deceive. Believe me, I should know, I've..."

"Screwed enough," I cut in.

"Only Eloisa," Potter came back at me angrily. "And doesn't that go to prove my point? She deceived me so she could go off and kill those children at the Wolf House. Then this so-called school teacher got me believing she was Kiera to delay me from reaching her. The wolves are nothing more than a bunch of murdering scum. Isn't it enough to know that Jack Seth betrayed you in the caves? You had your heart ripped out because of him."

"But..." I started.

"What is it with you and the wolves anyhow?" Potter cut over me, the snow now settling on the shoulders of the black coat he had put on. "It's almost as if you have a soft spot for 'em. It seems to me that it doesn't matter how many times they trick, deceive, and murder, you're still prepared to give them another chance."

"Bollocks!" I growled at him.

"You forget that not only did you die because of Seth, but Sparky murdered both your daughters – and yet you still give them the benefit of the doubt," Potter said, limping towards me. "You take the piss out of me because I've been seduced by a couple of wolves, but they fucked with my mind – what's your excuse, Sarge?"

I raised my fist to...to do what? Punch the man I loved as a son because he was speaking the truth? No, I couldn't do that. Potter stared straight back at me, unflinching.

"Why?" he asked me. "What is it with you and the wolves? Can't you see they are not to be trusted? They are nothing but lying, filthy scum, and I ain't going to stop until every single one of them is dead. Skin-walker, berserker, Lycanthrope, or any other kind of freaking wolf would all be dead if I had my way."

"You don't know what you're talking about," I breathed, lowering my fist. "Sometimes, Potter, you can't always help who you fall in love with." I then turned and climbed into the van and closed the door.

"What's that s'posed to mean?" Potter shouted as he came around the front of the vehicle to the passenger side and climbed in. He cried out in pain as he pulled himself into the seat.

"It means nothing," I said, starting the van.

"You're not in love with a freaking wolf, are you?" he groaned, and I couldn't tell whether it was in pain or disgust.

"Not me," I said thoughtfully, and rolled the vehicle slowly forward over the snow-covered road, the tyres making a muffled crunching sound in the night. "Okay. So let's say you are right about the boy, Sam."

"I am right," Potter cut in, taking another crumpled-looking cigarette from the equally crumpled-looking pack.

"We go and get Kiera, and then head for the Fountain of Souls," I said, steering the van through the snow.

"Can't this heap of junk go any faster?" Potter asked.

"With all the bitching you've been doing because you've got a few broken ribs, I didn't think you'd feel like flying," I barked.

"They will heal themselves in the next hour or two..." Potter started.

Then glancing sideways at him, I said, "If I'm right about Kiera and Seth, and you're right about Sam and Kayla, we don't have an hour or so while you heal up. Get some rest. Kiera's father's house isn't far from here."

Drawing on my pipe, I looked back through the windscreen, fearful of how much Kiera and Jack Seth now knew about each other's past. Perhaps nothing at all, but I doubted it somehow. This new world seemed to have the knack of *pushing* the past back together.

Chapter Five

Kiera

I went to the window and looked out. The night sky was almost white, bloated with snow-laden clouds. Apart from the wind that continued to buffer the side of the house, there was an eerie silence. Through the snow, I could just make out the church spire. Like the rest of the world beyond the window, it was covered white with snow, and it looked almost lost against the skyline. Somehow I felt trapped. Not by the room or the house, as I knew that I could leave at any time if I wanted to. I knew that I could just walk away, leaving Jack chained to the chair, my father stretched dead on the bedroom floor. But if I did that, I really would be trapped forever. There would be no resolution to this. Jack had said that Potter would come, he knew that. He had shown me the images of Potter with that teacher, Emily Clarke, and to think of them made my innards twist inside out.

I would wait for answers. I needed answers. Jack was secure. He was no threat to me or...

"How do you know Potter will come?" I whispered without turning to look back at Jack.

"He is going to be brought here," Jack said.

"Will he be hurt?" I asked.

"It all depends whether he came quietly or not," Jack said back, his voice flat, emotionless.

"He'll be hurt then," I said, knowing that Potter always put up a fight. With my back still facing Jack, I asked, "Is the photographer bringing him?"

"The photographer?" Jack asked, and I didn't need to look back to know he was smiling again.

"Whoever it was who took the picture of Isidor and Melody, whoever it was who took the picture of me and you downstairs while you were disguised as my father."

"Oh, that photographer," Jack said, sounding amused.

"Yes," I whispered.

"No, Potter won't be brought here by the photographer," Jack said.

I continued to look out of the window, the snow seesawing down on the other side of the dirty windowpane. "Those pictures were used to trap us, weren't they?" I said.

"You could think of them like that," Jack said. "Or perhaps they were to show you or remind you of what you once had, or in Isidor's case, what could have been. Perhaps Isidor is happy now?"

"He's dead," I said flatly, my stomach knotting again.

"Are you so sure of that?" Jack whispered as if teasing me, but I wasn't going to bite anymore.

"I saw the Skin-walkers rip his head off," I told him.

"That couldn't have been very nice to see," Jack said. Ignoring his flippant comment, I turned around and looked at him. "So how did the photographer do it?"

"Do what?" Jack smiled.

"Leave that picture for Isidor? The picture hadn't even been taken, right?" I said. "The picture of me and you as my father, Potter took that from my flat a few weeks ago, but yet, it was only taken tonight."

At first Jack began to chuckle to himself.

"What's so funny?" I asked him, starting to feel angry.

"I'm sorry," he said, the chains clinking around his wrists. "Thanks to you, I've had a very long time in this *pushed* world – so I guess I've had a chance to learn a lot more about it."

"So what have you learnt?" I asked him, wondering if he wasn't starting to play with my mind and heart again.

"The world is not as you understand it to be, little sister," he said, and now his smile had faded and he had taken on a more serious look. "Some people call them the 'slip-streams', others, 'cracks' and 'fault lines', but most call them the '*doorways*.'"

"What are you talking about?" I snapped at him impatiently.

"Some people call it *clicking, pushing, burrowing, falling, sliding*, but it all means the same thing," he said.

"What does?" I demanded.

"Passing between the different layers of this world," he said. "I've never been able to master it myself, never really wanted to, if I'm to be honest," he said with a slight sneer.

"What *layers*? What are you talking about?"

"There are many *layers*, Kiera, or should I call them *times* and *whens*?" he started to explain. "Some can pass between them, and others can't – or perhaps they can and just need a little *push!* I guess in the end, we all get *pushed* one way or another."

"What are you talking about?" I said, shaking my head.

"No one really dies," he grimaced, as he tried to reposition himself in the chair. "Dying is just like having the rug pulled out from beneath your feet when you least expect it. You fall away into another *time* or *when*. That's why some people call it *falling*. This world is just another layer that we've all fallen into. I'm guessing – although I can't be sure as I'm no expert on this – that this is how we've come to be in this new *world*. Don't you see? Isidor might be dead to you and your friends, but he is someplace else now in a different layer – time or when."

"I don't believe you," I hissed. "You're just trying to excuse his murder."

"I murdered you and we are both here together right now. Both of us are dead, *aren't* we?" Jack said.

"Well, yes..." I started.

"Well," Jack cut over me, "whoever is leaving those pictures might not be doing it to trap you, but to free you."

"Haven't you been listening to me!" I hissed. "Isidor is dead. How can that be a good..."

"You haven't been listening to me?" Jack shot back. "If this whole thing about different layers is true, then Isidor will be in another when, and perhaps this time with the person he truly loves and wants to be with. So maybe this photographer did a good thing!"

"And the photograph of me?" I sneered. "That led me to you! How is that a good thing?"

"You discovered the truth, didn't you?" he said, his eyes burning brightly. "However much the truth hurts, isn't it best to know it? Or perhaps you like living a lie? Knowing the truth about yourself will only help you make the right *choices* – the choices you need to make if you are going to survive in this *pushed* world. If it hadn't of been for that picture of you and your father, would you have ever sought him out here? Didn't that picture stir up all of those old memories and feelings that you had for him? It was that picture that brought you here. Did the photographer do such a bad thing if it led you to the truth – however painful that is?"

"But..." I started.

"But perhaps this photographer isn't your enemy," he cut in.

"Then who is it?" I said. "Why do they conceal themselves?"

"That, I don't know," he said with a shake of his head, and I got the sense that he was telling me the truth. If he had known, wouldn't he have wanted to have taunted me with that piece of information? "Whoever they are, they know how to click, slide, fall, and pass between the different layers – times and whens."

"Who will know the identity of the photographer?" I asked.

"The one who has truly mastered the art of..."

"What is their name?" I demanded, stamping my foot.

Then, before Jack had a chance to answer, the sound of a vehicle approaching broke over the noise of the wind outside. I turned and looked through the window. Crossing the room, I looked outside and down the hill. In the distance, I could just make out the shape of a van fighting its way through the snow and heading towards the house.

Potter? I wondered.

"Release me!" Jack suddenly shouted from the corner of the room, frantically rattling his chains. "You've got to let me get away from here." He sniffed the air.

"Why?" I asked, turning to look at him. "Isn't this what you wanted? Aren't these your wolves bringing Potter here?"

"There is only Potter..." Jack sniffed the air again. "...And *Murphy!*"

I looked back through the window. The van was halfway up the hill now. With my eyes no more than slits, I peered through the falling snow and the darkness. Jack was right! I could see Murphy hunched over the wheel of the van and Potter was sitting beside him. I knew then that whatever plan Jack had, somehow my friends had dashed it. But where were Kayla and Sam?

"Let me loose!" Jack howled.

"Why?" I said, turning on my heels to face him. "I thought this is what you wanted. We can at last all sit down and discuss with my friends what you have told me."

"They haven't come here to talk, Kiera," Jack howled. "They've come to kill me. They'll rip my throat out before I even open my mouth."

"They won't," I insisted.

"You know they will," he barked at me, struggling against the chains. "Murphy won't want you to know that he has lied and cheated you all this time. Potter isn't just going to sit there and let me tell you how he and Eloisa were once lovers – the true reason he ripped out her heart."

"If you're telling the truth, then you have nothing to fear," I told him. "Didn't you tell me that it was best to know the truth, however painful?"

"It's not the truth I fear," he barked at me. "It's your friends. They will take this chance to kill me. You have to let me go, Kiera – I'm your *brother*."

I looked back out of the window and could see the police van coming ever nearer. I turned away again and looked at Jack. "So this is my choice?" I whispered. "Do I choose you over my friends? Because if I set you free, Jack, there is every chance that you will come after them again – set another trap and kill them."

"Who do you choose, Kiera?" he said, the light going out of his eyes, that haunted look he had while telling me his story now masking his face again. "Which half of you do you choose? The Vampyrus or Lycanthrope?"

I shot a glance back over my shoulder and could see the van clearly now through the falling snow. Then, spinning around, I raced back across the room towards Jack. Leaning over him so my cheek brushed against his, I whispered in his ear and said, "I choose neither side." Then, with one quick swipe of my claws, I sliced through the chains and set Jack free. The chair toppled over as Jack sprang to his feet and headed towards the door. He yanked it open, then paused and looked back at me.

"You know I could have freed myself at any time, don't you?" he said. "At any point I could've changed into a wolf and broken free."

"So why didn't you?" I whispered.

"Because it had to be your choice, Kiera," he whispered back. "I had to know if you would save me over your friends."

"Why?"

"Because I had to know you believed me," he said softly.

"Believed what?"

"That I was your brother. I know you, Kiera. I know you are better than me. Despite what I've done to you, you couldn't let your brother die," he said, staring back at me. "At last I have what I've searched for my whole life."

"And what's that?" I breathed.

"Family," he smiled. Then, glancing briefly down at the man we had both once loved as a father, Jack fled the room.

With the sound of his feet thundering down the stairs, I raced after him. From the top of the staircase, I shouted, "Jack, what is the name of this person who understands how to pass between the different layers – times and whens?"

At the bottom of the stairs, Jack paused and looked back at me. With his eyes glowing fiercely in their sunken sockets, he said, "Her name is Lilly Blu. If you can find her – you'll love her!"

"Why?" I shouted.

"Because she's one of us," Jack grinned back at me. "Lilly's a wolf!" Then he was gone, racing out of the front door and into the night.

I ran back into the bedroom and to the window. I looked down to see Jack spring into the air, changing into a giant wolf in a blaze of glistening hair, claws, and razor-sharp teeth. Hidden by the trees which sat opposite the house, Jack turned on his giant paws and looked back at me. Throwing his head back, he released a deep, booming howl into the night. Then he was gone, leaving me alone at the window.

Moments after seeing Jack's long, bushy tail disappear between the black knotted tree trunks, the police van trudged to a stop outside, and I watched Murphy and Potter climb out. I couldn't help but feel anger and hatred for the both of them.

Chapter Six

Kiera

I sat in the chair, my father dead at my feet, and waited for Murphy and Potter. The lamp continued to shine its murky light from the corner. I took a deep breath and tried to gather my thoughts – gather my nerves – for the confrontation I knew was about to come. I heard the sound of the front door swing open below. The hinges made a wailing sound like a baby lost in the dark. There was a moment's silence.

"Kiera!" It was Murphy who called my name.

I didn't answer. I sat silently, taking shallow breaths. Tiny plumes of breath escaped my mouth and floated away into the dark.

"Kiera!" This time it was Potter who called, but his voice sounded laboured, as if in pain.

Again, I didn't answer.

I heard them moving around downstairs, and I tracked the sound of their footfalls as they passed from the living room, to the kitchen, and back again. Then, as I expected, I heard the clomping sound of their boots on the stairs, growing louder as they got higher. They stopped on the landing, just outside the door. There was a moment's silence, then the door came crashing open as Murphy came storming into the room, his long claws brandished before him. Potter stumbled in behind him. He looked stooped somehow, and one arm cradled his ribs. His face was covered in blood and the left side of his face was swollen out, black and purple coloured. His right eye was almost swollen closed, and the other was bloodshot. Murphy glanced around the room to see if there was any hidden danger.

Then, seeing me sitting in the chair with my father stretched out at my feet, he said, "Kiera, are you okay?"

"Where are Kayla and Sam?" I asked, ignoring his question.

His lips opened and closed as he fought to find the right words. "They're missing."

"Missing?" I asked.

"The teen-wolf has taken her," Potter mumbled from the open doorway. "I knew we should never have trusted a wolf. Scum, the lot of them."

"Scum?" I breathed, cocking my eyebrow at him.

"Yeah, scum," Potter wheezed. "Look what they did to me..."

"We'd better go and find them," I said, cutting Potter dead.

"Hang on a minute," Murphy said, looking down at my father. "What's gone on here? Who killed your father?"

"Jack Seth," I said, staring back at Murphy, searching his face for any flicker of emotion.

"See, nothing but murdering scum," Potter spat, shuffling away from the door towards me.

"Don't!" I barked, not looking at him, but raising my hand in the air, as if to warn him off. "Don't come near me."

"Why did he kill your father?" Murphy said, peering at me from beneath his bushy white eyebrows.

"Perhaps Jack killed him because my father killed his?" I said, refusing to take my eyes off Murphy.

Murphy glanced down at the body on the floor, and in that moment, I saw a flicker of recognition on his face, and that was all I needed to know Jack had been telling me the truth.

Although I could feel hot tears starting to burn in my eyes, I refused to shed them. I was too angry and hurt to cry.

With my eyes fixed on Murphy, I pointed down at my father's body and said, "To me he was Frank Hudson – my father. But to you he was known as Peter Murphy. He was your younger brother, wasn't he, *Jim*?"

Murphy raised his head and looked at me, and I could see not fear in his eyes, but sadness. "Yes, he was my brother," he whispered, then swallowed hard.

"Can someone tell me what the fuck is going on here?" Potter suddenly wheezed, then coughed, standing halfway between the open doorway and where I sat.

Then, turning to look at him, I whispered, "I'm scum."

"What that's s'posed to mean?" Potter said, hacking out a stream of coughs. He covered his mouth with his hand, but I could see the blood he had coughed up running between his fingers.

"All wolves are scum, right?" I glared at him.

"You know it," Potter said, wiping the blood from his hands onto his trousers.

"Then I must be scum, too," I said, unable to hold back the tears now. "I'm a wolf – half Lycanthrope."

"What's going on?" Potter said, glancing over at Murphy.

Dropping his head, so his chin almost touched his chest, Murphy said, "It's true."

"What a load of old bollocks!" Potter barked, his chest rattling. Then looking back at me, he added, "You can't be a wolf – you don't have a hairy tongue!"

I jumped up from the chair and said, "I can't deal with you right now, Potter."

"What have I done?" Potter groaned, pressing his hands against his ribs.

"*What have you done?*" I roared at him in disbelief. "How about you and that teacher? What about her?"

Potter looked at me, his eyes wide like a rabbit that had been caught in the headlights of a speeding car. "I thought that was you..." he started.

"Liar!" I screamed at him, tears streaming down my face. "I saw you! Jack showed me."

"That sonofabitch!" Potter shouted. "You've got to believe me, Kiera. She was a wolf. She did some of that mind-fucking with me."

"It looked like it was you who was doing all the *fucking!*" I hissed.

"It never got that far!" he yelled back at me, then took a deep breath as if refilling his punctured lungs. "I figured her out before anything like that happened."

"I'm surprised you didn't figure it out sooner," I sneered, wiping the tears from my cheek with the back of my hand. "Couldn't you feel her hairy tongue? After all, she had it shoved far enough down the back of your throat."

"You've got to believe me, Kiera," Potter said, shuffling towards me.

"Back off!" I spat, raising my hands. "Don't you dare touch me."

"I thought it was you – honestly," Potter said. "Jack Seth set me up. You saw only what he wanted you to see. He wants you to hate me."

"And what about Eloisa Madison?" I roared. "Was he lying about her, too?"

Potter looked at me as if he had been slapped across the face.

"It's true then?" I cried. "You and she were lovers – that's why you ripped her heart out!"

"I had sex with her once," Potter said. "It was before me and you ever met."

"So you killed her to stop me finding out," I said, glad that he was hurting.

"No!" he yelled at me. "I killed her because she was a child murderer. Just like that teacher and all of the other wolves – they have a way of getting into your head and messing with you. She tricked me into believing that someone else was the killer while she escaped. She looked into my eyes and made me forget about her. At first I did, but then I remembered. I remembered that night in the hangar just outside of Wasp Water. She was a danger to us – she was a killer. That's why I ripped her heart out."

"It's true," Murphy said from behind me.

I span around to face him, my fist clenched. "Why should I believe a word you tell me? You're nothing but a liar, too!"

"I've never lied to you, Kiera," Murphy said, and for once his voice wasn't gruff or angry sounding, it was soft. "I might have kept secrets. But I've never..."

"Secrets!" I gasped. "You've let me live a lie ever since I walked into your police station back in the Ragged Cove."

"I'm not proud of that fact," he whispered. "But I did it to keep you alive – just like I saved your life the day I plucked you from the dead waters."

"You tried to *drown* me!" I reminded him.

"You were already dead – or so I thought," Murphy tried to explain. "But the moment I heard your cries I went back for you – I saved you, Kiera."

"Can someone please tell me what the fuck is going on here?" Potter spluttered.

"*Shut up!*" both Murphy and I roared at him at once.

I turned back to face Murphy.

"I could have left you to die," Murphy continued. "But I didn't. I took you in my arms and..."

"Let me live a lie," I cut in.

"*No!*" Murphy insisted. "I kept you away from that woman – that wolf – Kathy Seth."

"My mother," I shot back.

"She wouldn't have been a mother to you, Kiera, not a *good* mother," Murphy said. "She would have destroyed you just like she destroyed Jack. The woman was pure evil. You've got to understand that. She would have ruined your life."

"My life has been ruined," I told him.

"Has it?" Murphy asked me. "You grew up with your father – my brother. He was a good man and loved you more than anything." He glanced over at the body on the floor, then back at me. "Jessica Hudson was a good woman, until Elias Munn destroyed her."

"And what about my brother – Jack?" I sniped.

"Brother?" Potter cut in.

I shot him a hard look, and he closed his mouth before saying anything else. I turned back to face Murphy. "You helped to make Jack what he is today."

"And don't you think I feel guilty about that?" Murphy said. "But I had my brother to think of. I know Jack was only a boy, but I couldn't risk him destroying the new life my brother had with you. But I tried to make amends."

"How?" I snapped.

"Years later when I arrested him for killing those women," Murphy started to explain. "The moment I saw him, I knew who he was. The curse might have eaten him up, made him look older, but I recognised him at once. I felt as if I had his victims' blood on my hands, too."

"How come?" I asked.

"Because perhaps you are right," he sighed deeply. "Perhaps I did help to make him the killer he is today. But that's the real trick. That's what the Lycanthrope are good at."

"They're good for something?" Potter groaned, collapsing into the seat where I had earlier chained Jack.

"Shut it, Potter," Murphy said gruffly. Then looking back at me, he added, "I did what I thought was best, Kiera. I did what I thought was best for you. But like I said, the wolves make you feel as if you have blood on your hands. The wolves have caused me nothing but heartache for as long as I can remember."

"What do you mean?" I asked him.

"I lied to Jack because I thought I was protecting my brother from..." he trailed off as if remembering something that had hurt him very much.

"From what?" I pushed, desperate to understand why Murphy had tricked Jack and kept secrets from me for so long. I wanted to understand so I didn't have to hate him.

"Although it pains me to say it, I do understand why Potter gave into those wolves like he did," Murphy said. Then, looking at Potter he said, "And there is a reason I keep giving the wolves a second chance. I freed Jack from prison because I felt guilty for what I had done. That is the truth of the matter." Murphy paused for a moment then swallowed hard. "To love a wolf is like no other love. They somehow take hold of you. You do stuff – take risks – give up everything you know to be right. I did what I did to try and save my younger brother."

"Save him from what?" I whispered.

"The pain of falling in love with a wolf and having your heart broken," he whispered back at me, his face looking suddenly grey and old. "I was in love with a wolf once, but no good came of it. It ended in heartache and murder."

Turning his back on us, Murphy went to the window. With one quick swipe of his claws, he pulled the curtains free. He crossed the room, and kneeling down, he covered his brother's body with them. Murphy lowered himself onto the chair and took his pipe from his trouser pocket. I sat on the floor, my back pressed against the wall, drawing up my knees beneath my chin.

With the wind howling outside and snow pelting against the window, I watched a cloud of blue smoke drift from the end of Murphy's pipe. His usually bright blue eyes looked clouded over and dark. Not looking at either Potter or me, Murphy looked thoughtfully ahead as he sucked on his pipe. Then slowly, he started to talk. This is what he said.

Chapter Seven

Murphy

I lived in a small house, deep in The Hollows with my mother and younger brother, Peter. My father had been one of those who had decided to go exploring in the vast wastes of the Talles Varineris canyon and had never returned. It was believed he had been transfixed by its beauty and had wandered into the canyon's great fissures and been lost forever. My mother had loved him deeply, and was never the same again. She suffered from melancholia and spent most of mine and my brother's childhood staring at the wall, as if unable to move or function until our father's return.

My brother and I were, therefore, often left to do as we pleased. Peter was more studious than I was and often spent his time with his head in books which had been brought down into The Hollows from the world above. He was interested in the art and the films made by the Vampyrus named Burton. I on the other hand, was interested by the world above, but not by the books and works of art – but by the adventures I hoped to find there. With my mother pretty much comatose most of the time, it didn't take much effort on my part to sneak away from home through the tunnels and the wells and out into the world above. I had found a tunnel which brought me out just on the outskirts of a great forest. You have to understand that for a boy of fourteen, this new world with its giant trees, lakes, and a sky that spread high overhead like a giant blue ocean was like climbing out of The Hollows into a fantasy land that promised adventure and excitement.

Like other young Vampyrus, I had heard the stories of the dangers that lie over our heads and how we should keep away from the humans because of their fear for anything different. I'd listened to the stories spread about by the Elders, that if the humans were to discover that a world of living, breathing winged creatures lived beneath them, they wouldn't be able to help themselves from coming below and capturing us – experimenting on us – killing us. But just like any human teenager, I thought I was immortal and that I would live forever. I never for one moment thought that I would ever face any danger or threat that could frighten me, let alone kill me. I believed I could take on the world.

My first few excursions above ground lasted only minutes, as I dared out of the tunnel I had found, and ventured into the new world I had heard so much about and was so desperate to explore. But with every trip above ground, my stays got a little bit longer. Ten minutes, twenty minutes, a full hour, half a day, then a full day and night. I didn't do much at first. I would tentatively wander into the forest, checking constantly back over my shoulder, checking that I could still see the hole that led back home should I need to head below ground quickly. As I grew more confident, I would sit and stare up at the sky and watch how the sun glinted and sparkled off the leaves of the trees which towered above. I could sit for hours on the forest floor, my back against the trunk of a tree and stare upwards, watching the clouds lumber lazily overhead. I'd sit there like that until my neck went stiff. As my confidence grew, I ventured further into the woods, until one day, I came across a vast lake. Its waters were red, almost black, and it seemed to stretch for miles in either direction. Never before had I seen such a thing. It was surrounded on all sides by fir trees and willow trees, which seemed to stoop over the lake as if taking a drink of water. I visited this lake every day for almost a year and never did I see anyone or anything other than my own reflection staring back at me from the dark red waters. Then one day, that all changed, and I spied the most beautiful creature I had ever seen.

The wolf came out from the shade of the trees, its paws gently trampling over the pebbles which covered the shore. Its long, sleek body was covered in fur so bright and golden, it looked like the wolf had somehow soaked up rays of the sun I had so often watched springing through the canopy of leaves in the forest. It came forward, sniffing the air as it approached me. Although my heart raced, it wasn't through fear, but wonder and curiosity. Along with the stories about the humans, I had also heard the stories of the murderous race known as the Lycanthrope. Surely such a beautiful creature as the one which stood before me couldn't be one of them. I had always imagined the Lycanthrope to be evil-looking monsters, with rows of jagged, flesh-infested teeth, and long, black, pointed tails and claws as ragged as a set of rusty nails. This creature looked nothing like those nightmarish images I had conjured. Its eyes shone as bright as its fur. The wolf circled me, making soft, short woofing sounds in the back of its throat. It's long, silk-like tail brushed against my legs, and I felt a tingle of excitement travel through my body. As the wolf circled me, it continued to sniff the air.

Eventually the wolf stopped, resting on its hind quarters before me. The creature was as tall as me, even though it was seated, and it looked straight into my eyes. At once, I felt almost overcome by a sense of warmth, joy – love? I couldn't be sure. I had never experienced such feelings before. My heart was beating so loud now, that it almost blocked out the sound of the lake lapping against the shore. Then the wolf spoke.

"You're not human, are you?"

The wolf's voice was soft, like that of a young girl. I was so surprised by it; I staggered backwards into the water.

"Be careful," the wolf spoke in warning.

This time I landed on my arse in the water. I splashed about as I tried to stand. Some of the red water went into my eyes and I wiped it away with the tips of my fingers. When I opened them again, the wolf was gone. In its place stood a young girl, who was about the same age as me. Just like the wolf had been the most beautiful creature I had ever seen, so was the girl now standing on the shore. Her feet were bare, but the skin looked soft and pearly white – something close to marble. The girl wore a pale blue dress which swished just above her knees. Thick golden locks of hair hung over her shoulders and her eyes shone a bright yellow. I had seen my fair share of pretty Vampyrus girls back home in The Hollows, and I had seen lovely-looking human girls in the picture books my brother often read – but I had never seen a girl as beautiful as the one who stood before me now.

"Are you going to stand there with your mouth open like that all day?" she laughed softly at me.

"Huh?" I asked.

"You're getting wet," she smiled, and it lit up her whole face. Then holding out her hand, she said, "Let me help you."

With my heart racing so fast now, I thought it might just go *bang,* I reached out and took her hand in mine. Her pale white fingers felt soft, yet brittle, as she closed them around my hand and gently helped me from the water.

"Come over here and sit in the sun," she said, guiding me gently towards a sandy patch of shore. "Your clothes will soon dry out."

I sat down beside the girl, not once taking my eyes off her.

"Are you okay?" she smiled.

"Sure," I said back. "Why?"

"It's just that you're staring at me," she giggled and looked away, out across the lake.

"I'm sorry," I stammered, my cheeks beginning to feel hot. "It's just that..." I trailed off.

"Just what?" she asked, glancing at me again.

"It's just that..." I paused, struggling to find the right words. "I've never seen a wolf before...what I mean is, I've never seen a real Lycanthrope before. You are a Lycanthrope, right?"

"Yes," she said with a nod of her head. "Do you have a problem with that?"

"No," I said. "Why should I?"

"Because you're a Vampyrus, aren't you?" she asked me.

I nodded and wondered how she knew. I had yet to reach the equivalent of human puberty and I was yet to shed my wings, fangs, and claws. I looked just like a human. "How do you know?"

"Your smell," she explained, twitching her nose at me with a mischievous smile.

"Thanks," I sighed.

"It's not a bad smell," she said. "But I've smelt it before."

"When?" I was curious to know.

"Once or twice, Vampyrus cops have come to the caves and snatched wolves they suspected of killing humans," she said, looking down at her hands as she passed a smooth-looking pebble between her fingers. "I recognised their smell on you."

"Oh?" I said, surprised. I'd heard the stories of the Lycanthrope killing humans, but I didn't know that there were Vampyrus cops who hunted them down.

"We shouldn't even be sitting here together," she said in a low voice. "Our two species aren't meant to mix."

"Why not?" I asked her, confused.

"I'm not sure why," she said thoughtfully. "I just know it isn't allowed. We could be punished."

I thought about this for a moment, then looking sideways at her, I said, "You haven't killed any humans, have you?"

"No, never," she said, sounding a little shocked.

"And I'm not a Vampyrus cop," I said. "So I don't see the harm in us sitting here together, do you?"

"I guess not," she smiled at me.

I smiled back at her, relieved that she didn't want to leave – not just yet anyhow. A silence fell between us. The girl looked back down at the pebble she passed between her hands, and I looked out across the lake. Feeling nervous and the heavy silence only making me feel more anxious, I finally said, "My name is James Murphy. What's yours?"

"I'm Penelope Flack, but everyone just calls me Pen," she said, looking at me again.

"Jim," I said back.

"No, not Jim, *Pen*, silly," she smiled.

"No, everyone just calls me, *Jim*," I laughed.

"Oh," she giggled, and the sound was so sweet. But it was her face – she was so goddamn pretty – especially when she smiled. Her nose sort of screwed up and her eyes sparkled like two twinkling suns. I thought she was the most perfect thing I had ever seen. How anyone could accuse the Lycanthrope of being a race of killers, I didn't know. The gentle-looking girl sitting before me looked like an angel, not a monster. The stories I had heard ever since I could remember about the wolves surely had to be wrong, I thought, as I sat and looked into her mesmerizing stare. But I was just a boy and I had a lot to learn – and that lesson would cost me more than I could have ever imagined.

Chapter Eight

Murphy

Pen and I became good friends, and if I were to be honest, my young heart felt more than that for her. It wasn't just because she was beautiful; my heart raced like an out-of-control steam engine every time I saw her – but it was her personality, too. Pen had a kind of innocence about her, and although she lived on the other side of the fountains, it didn't appear that she had ever ventured out into the human world. It was like something was holding her back. I often told her about what my home was like beneath, in The Hollows, the great canyons and the Light House which created the light and the darkness so we had something close to night and day. As we sat in the forest surrounding the lake, her mouth and eyes would be wide open as I told her about the vast tunnels, the seething volcanoes, and the great willow trees in the whispering woods. But what grabbed her attention most was the magical moving pictures the Vampyrus Burton had brought back below ground from the human world. At first she thought I was just messing with her.

"Pictures that move?" she breathed, one summer's afternoon as we lay on our backs in the grass, looking up at the wisps of cloud floating lazily overhead.

"That's right," I told her. "The human world is far more magical than even I first imagined."

"How come?" she asked, rolling onto her side and staring at me with her bright eyes, which were as yellow as the rapeseed which grew tall all around us.

"I saw these moving pictures once," I said, looking at

her. "This human girl and her dog discovered this other world, where there was a talking lion, scarecrow, and a man made of tin. There was this evil witch, too…"

"How did this human girl find this world?" Pen whispered as if in awe of what I was telling her. "Do you think we could go there and talk with this lion, scarecrow, and tin man?"

"There was this big storm and her house got sucked up into the sky," I explained, not really understanding it myself. "It was like this world had always been there – just like The Hollows beneath us and your world on the other side of the fountain. The girl, Dorothy was her name, found herself to be in this other magical world…"

"What was it called?" Pen asked, sitting up and crossing her legs beneath her dress.

"Oz," I told her.

"Oz," she breathed dreamily, as if trying to imagine it in her mind. Then looking back at me, she said, "Jim, are you sure you're not teasing me?"

"Honest," I said. "It really does exist. The humans captured it all in their magical moving pictures."

"I would love to see it one day," Pen said, a smile tugging at the corners of her lips.

"One day I will show it to you," I boasted.

"You promise?" she said, taking my hands in hers.

"I promise," I said, and she leant close to me and kissed me softly on the cheek.

I would have loved to have shown her Oz, but how? Then, by chance or by fate, I can't be sure, I heard that the Vampyrus Burton was coming back beneath ground for a short visit. Now Burton had become a bit of a celebrity in The Hollows, as every time he came home, he would have a whole new roll of moving pictures to show us. Vampyrus would come from every corner of The Hollows. This time, Burton returned with a stream of magical moving pictures that he had somehow captured. Just like the hundreds of other Vampyrus, I gathered in the great caves and Burton shone his moving pictures onto the rocky walls. There were cheers and gasps from the Vampyrus as we watched in wonder. Once the pictures stopped moving and the cave fell into semi darkness, I waited for the hordes of Vampyrus to leave as I hid in the shadows at the back of the caves. When Burton was alone, I crept from my hiding place.

"Who's there?" Burton asked, knocking his untidy black fringe from his brow.

"I want to go to Oz," I said, stepping into the light so he could see me.

With a smile on his lips, his wild, curly, black hair sticking out like springs all over his head, Burton looked at me and said, "And why would you want to go to Oz?"

"For the same reason that you did, I guess," I said back. "It's magical there, right?"

"Isn't there enough magic in The Hollows?" he asked me. But before I'd the chance to say anything, he added, "Anyway, it's impossible."

"I promised someone I would show them that magical place," I said, remembering the promise I had made to Pen.

"Who?" he asked, taking a step closer towards me.

"A friend," I told him. "I can't go back on my promise."

"You shouldn't promise something you don't truly understand," Burton said kindly.

"I can't let her down," I tried to explain.

"*Her*?" he asked with a smile.

"Yes, my friend, Penelope."

"Do you love this girl?!" He asked me, his eyes twinkling.

I looked at him, standing in the gloom, the *drip-drip* sound of water running down the cave walls. With my cheeks flushing red, I nodded and said, "Yes, I love her."

Burton came closer still. He snatched a quick look back over his shoulder at the cave entrance, then back at me. With his voice no more than a faint whisper, he said, "Bring your friend Penelope to this cave tonight. It has to be tonight as I go back above ground when the Light House turns south towards us."

"But I don't know if she will be able to..." I started.

"If you want to honour your promise, then be here tonight," Burton said, then turned and walked back to the equipment which shone the moving pictures onto the cave wall.

Without another word, I raced from The Hollows in search of Pen.

Although Pen and I had been friends for almost a year, we had yet to visit each other's homes. Pen said that she lived with her father, who distrusted the Vampyrus very much after they had wrongly arrested and imprisoned his brother for a crime he didn't commit. So she doubted I would be very welcome. I had been reluctant to invite Pen to my home deep within The Hollows because of my mother. My mum continued to flip between periods of darkness and light, although the darkness had consumed her more of late than the light. She would continue to sit for long periods – for days sometimes – and when things were very dark, for weeks at a time.

My younger brother Peter continued to spend his time with his head in books and had taken to reading the teachings of the Elders. He had fallen in with some others, who went twice weekly to worship the Elders at one of their many temples. Both Peter and I ran errands, cooked, and cleaned our tiny hollow as our mother sat, day after day, staring at the wall, waiting for the day my father would return. I guess, like Pen, although we rarely spoke about our parents, didn't really have a relationship with them. Pen had never said as much, but as she spent most of her time alone or with me in the forest, I guessed she had few friends of her own, and there was little to keep her at home. Just like Pen, my only true friend was her, and as for my mother...well...I would often sneak into her room and sit at her feet. I would gently stroke her hand or smooth down her hair, but mostly I sat in the shadows and watched her as she stared at the wall. Her eyes were like blank saucers, unmoving and unblinking. Her skin was white and hard-looking, as if chipped from alabaster and framed by a torrent of greying-black hair that hung dully around her shoulders. I loved my mum, but hated her all at the same time. I loved the memories I had of her from my younger years but detested the way she was now. In a strange way, I missed her, although she was always at home and never went anywhere. Although I didn't pray myself, I would often ask Peter to pray that our mother would just snap out of it, pull herself together and get over the loss of my father. I resented the fact she seemed unable to do this for the sake of Peter and me.

I found Pen by the edge of the great lake. Desperate to catch my breath, I reached her, and bending forward, I drew large mouthfuls of air into my lungs. When I could breathe again, I looked at her and said, "Pen you've got to come into The Hollows with me."

"When?" she asked looking a little startled.

"Right now," I wheezed, still out of breath from my run.

"I can't right now," she said, turning and heading back along the shore towards the Fountain of Souls.

"You must," I called after her.

"I have to get home. It's getting late and father will come

looking for me," she said back over her shoulder.

"Don't you want to see what Oz looks like?" I said.

At once, Pen stopped in her tracks. Then turning to face me, she said, "Really?"

I nodded with a smile. Pen smiled back, and then the smile faltered.

"I can't," she said.

"It has to be tonight or never," I explained.

Pen looked back over her shoulder at the flood of red water that raced upwards into the darkening sky.

"It won't take very long," I said. "Just an hour or two."

Pen looked back at me, and for the first time since meeting her, that bright yellow light which shone from her eyes looked weaker somehow. She looked afraid.

I held out my hand towards her. "There is nothing to be scared of," I said. "The Hollows are quite safe. I'll look after you."

"It's not The Hollows," she said, taking another quick look back at the fountain.

"What then?" I asked her.

Then, turning to face me again, she smiled, took my hand and said, "I haven't got long."

Chapter Nine

Murphy

Holding Pen's hand tightly in mine, I led her down into The Hollows. Every so often I would snatch a quick sideways glance and smile at the look of awe on her face. She seemed delighted by the bright green luminous moss that covered the walls and ground. She wondered up at the intricate network of tree roots that hung out of the sky. I heard Pen take a sharp intake of breath as she marvelled at the thousands of twinkling stalagmites which hung high above us, like stars in a jet-black sky.

"It's so beautiful," Pen whispered.

With a smile on my face, I snuck her through the maze of tunnels and towards the great caves where I hoped Burton would be waiting for us. When other Vampyrus came close, I held back in the shadows, clutching Pen's hand. It was forbidden for a Vampyrus to bring a Lycanthrope down into The Hollows, unless they were prisoners, brought below ground to face trial before the Elders. When they had passed on their way, we would sneak from the shadows and continue deeper into The Hollows. At last we came across the entrance to the great caves. They were in darkness, and I wondered if Burton had not tricked me in some way. With my heart racing, and hoping that I wasn't going to look a fool in front of Pen, I led her into the caves. It was then I saw a dim little light shining in the middle of the cave. Someone had lit a small fire, and its flames cast orange and red shadows across the walls. Pen gripped my hand as I led her towards it, the sounds of our footfalls echoing all around us. Then, as we drew near to the light, I could see that two small chairs had been positioned next to each other, facing the widest wall in the cave. There was a small table, too, and on it there had been placed a large clay bowl which was full of cooked Bree seeds. They smelt sweet – just like the popcorn the humans ate above ground. Next to the bowl had been placed two bottles of Inferno Berry juice. Now, that was rare and expensive stuff, only drunk by the richest Vampyrus. It was rumoured to come from a far-off land, and was therefore in short supply.

Guessing that it was Burton who had lit the fire, supplied the two chairs and the food and drinks, I looked at Pen and said, "Relax, take a seat."

I handed one of the bottles of drink to Pen and sat down beside her, the bowl of warm Bree seeds nestled between us. Pen took a handful and popped it straight into her mouth.

"It's delicious," she mumbled.

"I know," I smiled, seeing her happy face in the firelight.

Then, as if a whole new world was opening up before us, a huge square of light flickered onto the cave wall before us, and moving pictures started to play across it. From the moment Dorothy appeared onscreen and made her way up the dusty road to her aunt's farmhouse, Pen was transfixed. Occasionally, I would glance sideways at Pen and watch her hand delve into the bowl of Bree seed. As if on autopilot, her hand would blindly find her mouth and she would sit and munch on the Bree seed with her mouth wide open, not daring to take her eyes off the moving pictures. During various parts of the film, Pen would sing along as she quickly learnt the words to the songs.

"*You're off to see the Wizard, the wonderful Wizard of Oz. You'll find he is a whiz of wiz! If ever a wiz there was!*" Pen sang with a wide grin on her face.

I couldn't recall a time I had seen Pen so enthralled by

something. When the Scarecrow appeared, I began to sing along. "*I could while away the hours, conferrin' with the flowers, consulting with the rain. And my head I'd be scratchin' while my thoughts were busy hatchin', if I only had a brain...*"

Together we sat and held hands as we continued to burst into song throughout the length of the moving pictures. Pen's eyes and whole being appeared to sparkle. It made me happy to see my friend enjoying herself so much. As Dorothy finally made her way home to Kansas and the moving pictures stopped moving, I turned to Pen and said, "Did you enjoy it?"

"Did I enjoy it?" she gasped, her eyes bright and full of wonder. "Wouldn't you just love to wake up one day and find yourself in a place like Oz?"

"Well, yeah I suppose," I replied thoughtfully.

"Wouldn't it be great to be able to leave your old life behind, to go on an adventure? The only difference between me and Dorothy is, I wouldn't be rushing to get back home quite as quickly as she was," she said, looking at me.

"Why not?" I asked.

Then, jumping up so quickly that the bowl of Bree seed shot from her lap, Pen cried, "Oh no! I should be home already. I will be in trouble." Turning on her heels, and knocking her chair flying, she raced from the cave.

"Pen, wait!" I called after her. I raced towards the entrance to the caves, then stopped. Looking back over my shoulder and into the gloom, I said, "Thank you, Burton!"

"You're welcome," his voice echoed back at me from out of the darkness.

I caught up with Pen in the tunnels, and sensing her fear and dread, I took hold of her hand again as we raced up and out of The Hollows. Above ground it was night, although I didn't know exactly how late. We raced through the fields and towards the forest. At the treeline, Pen stopped and let go of my hand.

"Thank you, Jim," she whispered, as if fearing she might be overheard by someone or something.

"For what?" I whispered back.

"For keeping your promise and showing me the magical moving pictures," she smiled at me, but I could still see that fear in her eyes.

"What are you scared of?" I asked, keeping my voice low.

Then as if in answer to my question, I heard the sound of a deep booming howl coming from deep within the forest.

"That's what I'm scared of," she said, looking into the slices of darkness which stood between each tree trunk.

"Who is it?" I breathed, pulling her close. "What is it?"

"It's my father," she whispered, looking at me. "I have to go."

Then, without warning, she took my face in her hands, and kissed me. Her lips felt soft, and her tongue even softer as she slipped it into my mouth. Unable to resist the urge, I kissed her back, wrapping my arms around her. I pulled her so close it was like we had become one. My heart roared inside my chest, my legs felt weak, and my head spun. We kissed long and slowly, then fast and passionately, as she ran her fingers through my untidy hair. In truth we only stood by the edge of the forest and kissed for no more than mere moments, but to me it felt like forever.

The sound of the howling and snarling came closer, and Pen slowly pulled away. She let go of my hand and stepped towards the treeline.

"Go," she said, looking back at me.

"I can't," I told her with a dumb smile spread across my face, feeling as if I'd just woken from a dream.

"It's not safe for you. Now go!" she snapped.

"I'll meet you tomorrow then," I said.

"No," she said.

"No?" I asked curiously. "But we've just kiss..."

"That must never happen again," she whispered.

"Why not?" I said, still feeling delirious.

Then, looking back at me from the darkness, her eyes bright, Pen said, "We can never be together, Jim."

"Because I'm a Vampyrus and you're a Lycanthrope?" I asked, what she was saying now slowly starting to slice through the euphoria I felt from being kissed by her.

"Yes," she said, with a slow nod of her head.

"But we could run away," I said, stepping towards her and reaching for her hand again.

"No," she hissed, looking back over her shoulder at the sound of the howling that was growing ever nearer.

"Why not?" I almost pleaded, taking hold of her hand and never wanting to let go.

"Because my father would kill me," she whispered, slipping her hand from mine. Then Pen was gone, disappearing into the darkness and out of sight.

"But I love you," I whispered.

"I know," I heard her whisper, which was drowned out by the sound of snarling and barking. I screwed up my eyes, desperate to get another glimpse of her, my heart aching. But I couldn't see Pen however much I tried, and I didn't see or hear from her again for another seven years.

Chapter Ten

Murphy

Over the following seven years, I heard and saw nothing of Pen. During that time, my mother fell ever deeper into her catatonic state and reluctantly, Peter and I had agreed to place her into the care of the Black Coats who carried out charitable work within and above The Hollows. Here, our mother would be cared for full-time. As my brother spent more and more of his time preaching the word of the Elders, he got to see my mother often. Peter explained to me that he wanted to spend his life dedicated to the teachings of the Elders and he finally became a Black Coat himself, taking a ministry above ground in the human world. Peter would spend his time relocating the Lycanthrope who were trying to beat their curse. It was during this time, while listening to Peter talk of his work, I came to understand the conflict the Lycanthrope fought with inside of themselves. I became aware of the murderous acts that they carried out against the humans and their children. Like my brother, I too wanted to help if I could, but not by devoting my life to a bunch of ghosts like he had. I'd often heard about the Vampyrus who had infiltrated the human police and then gone on to hunt down and capture the Lycanthrope who gave into their curses and murdered the humans. I thought that I would be doing some good if I did that. Like Peter, I had a deep sense of what was right and wrong, but I just wanted to express it in another way - I wanted some excitement and an adventure, too.

Although I had ventured above ground many times, I still knew very little about the humans and the way they lived.

If I was going to police them, I would have to understand them better. So on my eighteenth birthday, I left The Hollows, only returning when the thirst was upon me, and made my way in the human world. I floated from job to job and from town to town, watching and learning from the humans. If I fucked up and feared that they had become suspicious of me, I would move on. After a year of living something close to a nomadic existence, I found myself a job in a small record store. It was while working here that I met Chloe. She was a human and I learnt a lot from her – but more than that, she helped me forget Pen.

How to describe Chloe? She was beautiful. Not like Pen – completely different – and not just because she was human. She was gentle and kind and so much fun to be with. Chloe saw the fun in everything, and although we were two different species, I could almost be myself with her. She had no idea what I truly was, and when I did have to return to The Hollows to rid myself of those cravings, I told her I was visiting my sick mother – which wasn't a complete lie. Every time I went home I would go to mother, brush her hair, sit by her feet, and hold her hand while she sat and stared blankly at the wall. I would talk to her about Pen, but gradually the conversations became less about her and more about Chloe.

By the age of twenty-one, I finally felt confident enough in the human world to fulfil my ambition of joining the police force. With the extra money, Chloe and I made enough to rent a small house together on the edge of town. We were more than just friends by that time, we had become lovers, and Pen and that kiss we had shared together was nothing more than a distant memory – or so I thought.

One morning, I picked up the letters from the doormat and carried them through to the kitchen. Chloe was still in bed, it was Saturday, and she wanted to lie in. As the kettle boiled away in the corner, I thumbed through the letters, most of which were nothing more than junk mail. Then, at the bottom of the pile, there was an off-white envelope. My name had been scribbled across the front, but there was no address or post stamp. I placed the other letters to one side, and sitting down at the kitchen table, I opened the envelope. I took out the letter, feeling as if I had been slapped across the face. The letter was from Pen, and this is what it said:

Dear Jim,

How are you? That's a dumb question, right? But you have no idea how many times I have started this letter, then ripped it up and started all over again. So, I'm just going to write everything down. So here goes...

...Sorry it has taken me so long (seven years? Has it really been that long?)to get in touch but things haven't been easy for me since we last saw each other that night.

Firstly, I want you to know that I'm well, happy, and safe and I miss you – always have – how could I forget you? My father had somehow found out about my friendship with you. So he sent me away. Remember I told you about his brother – the one who was imprisoned by the Vampyrus for a crime he didn't commit, well he got out and my father sent me to live with him. My father just dumped me on him. I don't think he was expecting me. Uncle John was pretty cool about everything. He was a pretty cool guy all round, really, and I think that perhaps he was innocent. Whatever he might have or not done, he just took me in and gave me a home. I saw very little of my father, and like most Lycanthrope, he seemed to struggle with the curse. So John became more of a father to me than an uncle, and I loved him as one.

However, two years ago John died. He came home late one night with a fatal injury. I don't know what had happened – a fight perhaps? I never really knew what he got up to and there is a part of me that never wants to know. But he died in my arms in a pool of his own blood on the kitchen floor. It was a very difficult time for me as I had grown to love him very much. Although life has sometimes been tough, what so often got me through, was remembering that night we spent together in The Hollows. I often think back to that world you took me to – not just The Hollows – but Oz. Although I don't think I could ever return to my world beyond the Fountain of Souls, I have created a little piece of Oz in the human world!

My uncle left me a sum of money – I do not know how he came by it and I think it is best not to know. But with it I have invested the money and opened a little café and bar, which I have named the 'Wizard of Ooze.'

Why don't you come and stay? I'm desperate to see you again. We could hang out like we did before. It'll be just like the old times, me and you.

Write back (the address is at the top of the letter) would love to hear from you!

Miss you Jim!
Your friend,
Pen

With my heart thumping in my chest, I read the letter over and over and was so pleased to know that Pen was safe and well. I then folded it, placed it back into the envelope, and tucked it into my trouser pocket. I couldn't risk Chloe reading it. Not just because it was from another woman, but because it spoke of The Hollows, the Fountain of Souls, and what Pen and I really were – a Vampyrus and a Lycanthrope. I wrote back at once and told her everything. I explained how much I had missed her, and spent so much of the last seven years wondering what had happened to her. I wrote about my mother and brother, then told her I had joined the police force. With the pen poised over the paper, I looked up at where Chloe still lay asleep above me. Then, taking a deep breath, I wrote that I had met a girl called Chloe and how much I loved her. I hoped that Pen would understand and still want to see me. Once dressed, I left the tiny house I shared with Chloe, and posted the letter to Pen. As I walked back to the house, all of those feelings I had once felt for Pen came rushing back through me. I could vividly remember all those lazy afternoons we had spent together, the night we had spent in The Hollows, and that kiss we had shared. It was that kiss I kept playing over and over in my mind as I tried to crush the feelings it had woken inside of me.

Back at the house, I found Chloe wearing her night dress and sitting at the kitchen table. She had a steaming mug of coffee in one hand.

"Okay, honey?" she smiled. "You don't look well – like you've seen a ghost or something."

I sat down at the table across from her and told her all about Pen. Not everything, you understand. Not about The Hollows, the Fountain of Souls, the Vampyrus and the Lycanthrope – but just about a childhood friend who wanted me to go and visit. As I sat and spoke, that kiss came to the forefront of my mind again and whatever feelings that Pen's letter had stirred inside of me, I knew that I had better get a grip of them real quick. Not just because it was unfair to Chloe to be harbouring such feelings for another – but I was a cop now and any mixing between the Lycanthrope and Vampyrus was forbidden.

Chapter Eleven

Murphy

I received another letter from Pen about a week later, giving me the address of her café-bar. She said that she was happy for me that I had found love with Chloe and invited her along too for the grand opening of her café. Pen explained in her letter that we both had to come dressed as characters from the moving pictures, 'The Wizard of Oz.' I went dressed as a scarecrow and Chloe as the wicked witch.

'The Ooze Bar' was packed on its opening night. The place was full of Tin Men, Scarecrows and Lions. Holding Chloe's hand at my side, I looked about the café in search of Pen. What would she look like now, seven years later? Would I recognise her? Was she in costume like the rest of us and would she recognise me? I felt nervous but excited all at the same time at the thought of seeing her again. I looked around the café and to see all of those tin men, lions, witches, and scarecrows reminded me of the night we sat and watched the magical moving pictures together. There was a real carnival type atmosphere in the place and it buzzed with pulsating music and energy. Then, without warning, a pair of hands slipped over my eyes from behind.

"Guess who?" a voice whispered in my ear.

I whirled quickly around and there she was, dressed like Dorothy from 'The Wizard of Oz'. Despite the long platted pigtails, which I guessed was a wig, I recognised that smile pulled across her face, her bright hazel eyes. Pen looked older, but more beautiful than I had remembered. Her body had grown up, too, and filled out in all the right places.

"Wow, you've grown up!" I said.

"So have you! Filling out nicely I see," Pen grinned, patting my stomach. "Good to see you again, Jim."

"You too," I smiled, my heart leaping, as I hugged her tightly in my arms.

Letting go of her, I turned to look at Chloe. "This is Chloe," I told Pen.

"Hello, Chloe," Pen smiled.

"Hi," Chloe said back, and even beneath her bright green make-up I could see she felt uncomfortable.

If I were to be honest, I felt uncomfortable, too. I was unfamiliar with Pen's new friends. As we sat and chatted at the end of the bar and watched the inhabitants of Oz jive around the small dance floor, Pen beckoned over one of her staff. I guessed she was in her early twenties, just like us, but it was hard to tell behind the heavy lion's make-up that she was wearing. She had light blond hair which had been vigorously backcombed to resemble a lion's mane.

"This is Annie," Pen shouted over the booming music.

"Pleased to meet you, Annie. I'm Jim," I said. "This is Chloe."

"Good to meet you both," Annie said as Pen propped her arm around her shoulder.

"Annie's a real sweetheart, she keeps me out of trouble," Pen said wistfully.

"Pen's told me all about you," Annie said as if studying me. "She said you were like a brother and sister once."

"I guess we were," I said, looking at Pen.

"She doesn't stop talking about you!" Annie smiled. *"Jim, this and Jim that!"*

"I have the same problem," Chloe chipped in, staring at me. "I've heard so much about Pen, I didn't know what to expect!"

"Am I a disappointment?" Pen asked, flamboyantly

tossing her Dorothy style pigtails from side to side.

"Mmm...let me think about that for a moment!" Chloe placed one hand to her chin and pondered.

I couldn't tell if Chloe was joking or not.

"That witch's costume suits you," Pen suddenly teased Chloe. "I bet you didn't have to borrow a broomstick, you brought your own!"

Chloe looked at Pen, and with a wry smile on her green lips, she said, "I borrowed yours!"

There was a moment's silence between them and I wondered if they would get on or not. Then, both of them began to laugh. I hoped Pen and Chloe would grow to be friends.

Annie said farewell and went back to serving the customers that were queuing at the bar.

"Annie's been a good friend to me," Pen said. "I met her a year or so ago. I worked for a local photographer. Weddings, that sort of thing. I never took any pictures. It was my job to try and get people to have photographs taken of their kids. We had a stall set up in the local shopping mall, taking kiddie photos for ten pounds a go. Anyway, Annie comes along with this doll of a girl in a pram. My boss gives her the hard sell – telling her what a beautiful kid she's got and it would be a crime not to have her picture taken. I could see that she really didn't want to have it done – she didn't look as if she had ten pennies to rub together let alone buy a photo. But my boss just keeps ragging on at her, until she gave in.

"He's sounds like a real nice guy," Chloe added.

"He was okay, just under pressure to make money, you know," Pen said with a shrug of her shoulders. "Anyway, she has the picture taken, and although the photo wouldn't be developed and sent to her for a few days, she has to pay up front. I'm working the register and see this all going on. She reluctantly comes over to me, opens her purse, and hands me the money in a five pound note and the rest in change. I take a peek in her purse and can see that this leaves her with nothing. I took down her address so I could post the picture to her a few days later."

"Didn't you feel guilty?" Chloe asked.

"I didn't stop thinking about her for days. I wondered if her kid was going hungry or going without because we had taken her last ten pounds. So when the picture was ready, instead of mailing it out to her, I personally went round to deliver it. She lived in this scruffy-looking apartment block just outside town. I handed over the picture to her along with her ten pounds. But she refused to take it, she was too proud. So once she had gone back inside, I posted the ten pounds through her letterbox. As I was walking away, she came to the door and called me back. 'Jeez, you are persistent,' she said. She invites me in for a coffee and that was that, we became good friends."

"What about a partner? Where was her daughter's father?" I asked.

"Hit the road, as soon as he found out he was gonna be a daddy," Pen explained.

Chloe shook her head and said, "Loser."

"Yeah, I know," Pen agreed. "It's his loss. Katie's a real cutie, a peach of a little girl. Anyway, I started going round to see Annie and sometimes we would take Katie to the park. Anyway, we would sit and talk and I would tell her how one day, I would own my own café. I promised her that if my dream ever came true, I would give her a job."

"And here she is," Chloe said as she glanced over at Annie who was laughing with a customer.

"That's right. She might only be bar staff at the moment, but as I get on, so will she," Pen said.

"Who looks after Katie while she's at work?" I asked.

"I pay her a little more than the rest, you know to cover the cost of a babysitter," Pen explained.

"That's really sweet of you," Chloe said.

"I know," Pen smiled.

Pen's opening night was a huge success. Just before she closed for the night, Pen announced the winner of the fancy-dress competition. The winner was a guy in his early twenties, and he'd won a bottle of champagne. I got the feeling that Pen didn't choose him because he was the best costume, but because he was probably the best looking. The winner looked to be very drunk, as he smooched away on the dance floor with Pen to *'Somewhere Over the Rainbow'*, while the entire bar cheered and roared with good-natured laughter. I watched as Pen pulled the guy close and I felt a sudden stab of jealousy in my guts. Pen looked at me over the guy's shoulder and smiled at me.

Chloe and I hung around until the last of the drinkers had staggered out into the night and Pen had locked the door behind them.

Pen turned to me, and beaming, she said, "Jim, I've done it. I've actually done it! I've escaped my past life and have a whole new world." With a mischievous glint in her sparkling eyes, Pen laughed and said, "I'm the Wizard of Ooze!"

I couldn't remember seeing her happier.

Chapter Twelve

Murphy

I didn't see Pen after that night for a whole year. This wasn't because I hadn't wanted to; it was more of a matter of circumstance. I had been very busy that year at work and Chloe had decided to become a paramedic. What, with us both working alternate shift patterns, I was often climbing out of bed as she was getting in. Any free time we had became quite precious, so we usually spent this together, enjoying one another's company.

Pen had been very consumed throughout the year trying to make 'The Ooze bar' a success. I think even she had been surprised at how much work was involved in running your own business. Even though we hadn't managed to get together, we still spoke a couple of times a week on the phone and we still enjoyed writing each other the occasional letter.

It was in one of these letters, Pen told me that she was living with a guy. In the same letter, she also invited Chloe and me to stay with her over Christmas.

The weather, as usual for that time of year, had been awful, and our progress to Pen's that Christmas Eve had been slow-going. Huge waves of snow had cut across the roads, hampering our view ahead. Chloe had brought with her a collection of Christmas songs on CD and we wiled away the hours, keeping ourselves full of festive spirit by singing along to them.

We finally arrived at Pen's just past 2 a.m. on Christmas morning. Pen was waiting up for us with two large mugs of hot chocolate at the ready. Once we had dragged our bags into the hallway, we sat in the lounge and talked in the glow of the Christmas tree lights that winked on and off.

"What do you think to the Christmas tree?" she asked as Chloe and I warmed ourselves.

"It's huge," I replied. Looking at its long branches and being reminded of the fir trees that had surrounded the great lake and its dark red waters.

"I had to cut the top off, just to get it into the house," Pen laughed to herself.

"You've certainly done the house up wonderfully," Chloe said, glancing around the room at the mass of decorations that hung from the ceiling.

"Marc helped me," Pen said.

To hear of the guy's name made my stomach ache with jealously again – or was it regret that it wasn't me?

"Sorry he didn't wait up to meet you, but he's gone to bed," Pen added.

"So, he's living here with you?" I asked, trying to sound casual and matter-of-fact.

"Yeah, he moved in almost right away," Pen explained, but wouldn't make eye contact with me.

"Must be love," Chloe smiled, then glanced at me.

"He is kinda cute. We hit it off almost straight away," Pen told us.

"So how did you meet?" Chloe asked.

"He just strolled into the bar one day looking for a job. I had just lost a barman and Marc said he had done bar work before – so I hired him there and then. He seemed to know what he was doing and got on well with the customers. He began to suggest a few ideas of how the café could run better."

"Like what?" I was curious to know as it appeared to me that Pen's café had been running just fine before this Marc suddenly appeared on the scene.

"Marc suggested that I start serving breakfast, you know nothing too much, eggs, bacon, and toast – that sort of thing. I was lucky really because his brother happened to be a chef and Marc thought it would be a good idea to hire him."

"So they're both working for you?" Chloe asked, shooting me another look with her dark brown eyes.

"Yep, Steve works in the kitchen and Marc is now my bar manager," Pen explained.

"Bar manager? He's been promoted through the ranks rather quickly," I said.

"Wait 'til you meet him, he's a nice guy," Pen assured the both of us.

"I can't wait," I said, looking straight back at her.

I was woken to the sound of 'Mary's Boy Child' by Bony M playing on the radio somewhere in the house. I peered at my watch and groaned when I read that it was only just after 7 a.m. Chloe and I hadn't crawled into bed until the early hours, as we had sat up talking with Pen.

I rolled over and nestled my head against Chloe's auburn-coloured hair.

"Merry Christmas, Chloe," I said and kissed her cheek.

"What time is it?" she murmured without stirring.

"Just gone seven," I told her.

"Aw, it's still the middle of the night," Chloe groaned, pulling the bedding tighter about her shoulders.

"C'mon, sleepyhead, it's Christmas day," I said, gently shaking her.

"Okay, Okay, what's the rush?"

"Firstly, I want my present…" I started.

"Who says you're getting one?" she murmured.

I ignored her teasing and continued. "And secondly, I'm dying to meet this Marc."

"Mmm…he sounds rather intriguing. Pen seems to be hooked on him," she said, still sounding half-asleep.

"I just hope she isn't being used," I wondered aloud.

"What d'you mean?" Chloe rolled over onto her back and looked at me through a pair of half-opened eyes.

"I dunno. Call it a copper's nose, call it a hunch, but something just doesn't feel quite right." I swung my legs over the edge of the bed and got up. Chloe rolled over again as if to go back to sleep, so I grabbed one of the pillows and dropped it on her head.

"C'mon, I want my present," I laughed.

"Your present is at the end of bed," she groaned.

I looked down to see a brightly wrapped box. Excitedly, I removed the wrapping paper and the box lid and looked inside. "Carpet slippers?" I frowned.

"Don't you like them?" she asked, peering over the top of the bed covers at me.

"I guess," I said, looking at them.

Then, giggling, she whispered, "I've got your present right here." Chloe pulled back the bedding to reveal her naked body.

"Happy Christmas, Jim," I whispered to myself in delight. Dropping the slippers, I dived on top of her.

Squealing with pleasure, Chloe yanked the duvet over us, where we stayed together for another hour or so.

We showered, dressed, then made our way downstairs. Pen and Marc were already up and were cuddled up together on the couch by Pen's enormous Christmas tree.

"Merry Christmas," Pen beamed.

They both got up from off the couch. "Marc, this is Jim and Chloe."

Marc stuck out his hand and we both shook it warmly in

turn.

"Good to meet you at last," I said, looking into his eyes. They were a bright hazel-orange and I knew, like Pen, he was a Lycanthrope.

"Likewise, I've heard so much about the pair of you, particularly you, Jim," Marc said.

"All good I hope." I knew it was a bit of a lame reply but it was all I could think of saying. Marc was, I guessed, in his late twenties. He was slim, tall, with light brown hair that dangled across his forehead. He wore a hooped earring in his left ear and had a short goatee beard.

"While you sit and get to know each other, I'll go and get the champagne," Pen said excitedly.

"Champagne? What's the special occasion?" I asked Marc as Pen left the room.

"It's *Christmas*, isn't it?" he grinned, taking his seat back on the couch.

Chloe snuggled up cosily into a large armchair and I sat on the rug by her feet.

"Pen told us that you're working at the café," I said in an attempt to break the silence.

"Actually, I'm the bar manager," he said in a way that right from the start illustrated his importance in Pen's life and business.

"Yeah, she told us that," I said nonchalantly as if it made no odds to me whatsoever. "What did you do before?"

"Before what?" Marc asked as if knowing what I was getting at.

"Before you met Pen?" I said, staring at him.

"This and that, all sorts of stuff, really," he smiled back at me.

"Oh yeah, like what?" I tried to ask as casually as I could.

"Boy, when Pen said you were a cop, she wasn't

kidding," Marc tried to joke.

"What do you mean?" I asked.

"It feels like I'm under interrogation." Marc attempted to make this sound like a joke, but I knew he was really telling me to fuck off.

"How would you know what it feels like to be interrogated?" I pressed with an insincere smile playing on my lips.

He stared at me momentarily, those bright eyes of his weighing me up. Pen entered the room carrying a tray of glasses filled with champagne.

"Everyone's hitting it off, I hope," she said.

"We're all getting along just fine," Marc smiled back at her.

Pen handed out the glasses, then raised hers into the air. "A toast to new friends, new beginnings, and a very merry Christmas!"

We all stood and 'clinked' our glasses together.

"Merry Christmas," Chloe and I said.

"Merry Christmas," Marc grinned, raising the glass to his lips and taking a sip, and all the while eyeing me from over the rim of it.

Chloe and I made a move back home the day after Boxing Day. I had enjoyed the last few days spent with Pen. Although Marc and I hadn't really hit it off, we remained polite and civil to one another but I got the feeling that he didn't like me. I wasn't bothered as I didn't trust him. I just couldn't put my finger on it, but something just didn't seem to sit right with him, and it wasn't just the fact that he was a Lycanthrope.

"Are you sure you're not jealous?" Chloe asked me as I attempted to explain the nagging feelings of concern I had.

"Jealous, what do you mean?" I asked, secretly

wondering if that wasn't the real reason for my dislike of Marc. "Why would I be jealous?"

"Aw c'mon, Jim," Chloe sighed with a smile, as we set off in the car for home. "She's a beautiful woman and I guess she always has been – even back when you were just a couple of kids. Do you seriously expect me to believe that you didn't have a crush on her?" Then fixing me with a cool stare, she added, "And perhaps you still have?"

"Nonsense," I said, shaking my head. "We were like brother and sister – that's all it was back then and now. I'm not jealous. I'm happy for Pen if she's met someone who's good for her and will make her happy. I just get the feeling that Marc isn't going to do that for Pen."

"Why not?" Chloe asked, still watching me.

"Dunno," I sighed. "Just something…"

"Pen will be okay. She's all grown up now. You both are, you're not fourteen anymore," she said, steering the car along the narrow country roads, which were still heavy with snow.

"I know…I know…" I said thoughtfully, sitting back in my seat and watching the world that I had come to call my home, speed past outside.

Chapter Thirteen

Murphy

Come spring, I had managed to secure myself a secondment to 'The Special Operations Department' (or Special Ops as it was commonly known) at work. I was therefore no longer carrying out uniform patrol and spent most of my time working undercover, undertaking covert observations on drug dealers and armed robbery suspects. I had my Inspector to thank for such a rapid progression in my career. Like me and the other officers on his team, he had handpicked all of us, because we were like him – we were all Vampyrus.

Part of my new role involved me setting up 'stings' to capture the rogue Lycanthrope who were committing crimes in our county. As part of this team, I learnt how to track them; to hide secret cameras to help locate the wolves and capture not only them, but their crimes on tape. This would be undisputable evidence that would eventually determine the wolf's fate when taken down into The Hollows and tried before the Elders.

These were extremely dangerous operations and the risk to the undercover officer's life was high. If the intended target became suspicious in any way, which had happened on several occasions before, the Lycanthrope would show no hesitation in killing the Vampyrus cop. I therefore had to become extremely skilled in secreting the cameras so they were not obvious or visible to the wolf we tracked. The cameras that I used were known as 'pin-hole cameras', the idea being that they were so small they could actually be hidden in the pin-hole on the lapel of a suit jacket, in a book, in a car, or hotel room. I became quite skilled and cunning in my deployment of these cameras and would hide them in the faces of television sets, in alarm clock faces, behind two-way mirrors, and even in the ceiling right above a bed where the Lycanthrope intended to murder his human victim.

As I was very busy with work, I hadn't seen Pen since Christmas. We continued to speak on the telephone and exchange letters. Pen always listened with interest as I enthused about my job, but she said very little. I guess it was difficult to listen to me babble excitedly on about how I spent my time hunting down her own kind and sending them to trial down in The Hollows.

When I asked Pen how 'The Ooze Bar' was doing, I noticed she was often reluctant to elaborate on her business and even more secretive when I asked about Marc. Again, I often felt that sense of unease about Marc. So, when my Inspector authorised me a few days leave that Easter, I took the opportunity to go and visit with Pen. Unfortunately Chloe was unable to get holiday from work, so I went on my own. On Good Friday morning, I threw a packed bag into the boot of our car and began the long drive to Pen's.

As soon as Pen opened her front door, I could see she had lost weight and looked tired.

"How ya doing?" I asked, pulling her close to me and hugging her tight. I was shocked at how bony she felt in my arms.

"I'm good," she tried to assure me.

I followed Pen into the living room and could see that her jeans were hanging loosely about her hips due to so much weight loss.

"Have you been dieting?" I asked casually.

Pen looked herself up and down then back at me. "Aw,

no I haven't. I think it's the long hours I've been doing. It's hard work running the café. I always seem to be rushing about and I'm on my feet from morning 'til night."

"Where's your bar manager, doesn't he help out?" I asked, trying not to sound resentful or jealous.

"Yeah, he does...he's at the café at the moment with his brother getting everything ready for opening tonight. Anyway, can I get you a Coke or anything?" Pen said, trying to steer me away from the topic of Marc.

"That would be great, thanks."

Pen disappeared into the kitchen and returned within moments and handed me my drink.

"I've got something to show you. Come with me," she said excitedly. I followed Pen upstairs to her bedroom, the place she slept with Marc, I guessed. She swung open the door and said, "Well, what do you think?"

I stepped into the bedroom and in the far corner was a tall glass cabinet. I walked towards it and could see it contained statues and memorabilia from 'The Wizard of Oz.' I took a closer look. There were porcelain models of Dorothy, Tin Man, Scarecrow and the Lion, displayed neatly on glass shelves. There were pictures, but the jewel of this collection was a pair of sequined ruby slippers.

"Do you like it?" Pen whispered.

"Well, yeah...you certainly love Oz, there's no doubt about that," I smiled at her.

"Are you mocking me?" she smiled back.

"Would I mock you, Pen?" I laughed, although I was a little curious as to why she had collected all this stuff.

As if reading my mind, Pen looked at me and said, "I've never been able to forget that night you took me down into The Hollows and we watched those magical moving pictures."

"I haven't been able to forget it either," I whispered,

looking into her eyes. "I couldn't forget how you left that night."

"I didn't want to go," she said. "I wish we had grown up together for longer. Perhaps..." Pen trailed off.

"Perhaps what?" I pushed.

"We would be together now," she breathed.

"We are together now," I said.

"You know what I mean," she came back at me, her eyes looking haunted somehow.

"And you know that it would've never worked out between us, however much we might have wanted it to. It is forbidden for us to mix," I reminded her.

Pen stood silently for a moment, staring at the red ruby slippers in the glass case. "Do you remember the kiss?" she finally asked, without looking at me.

"How could I forget it?" I whispered.

Then, turning to face me, she whispered, "Do you want to kiss me like that now?"

"Yes," I nodded slowly.

"Why don't you then?" she whispered back, taking a step forward so she brushed up against me.

"Because it's not allowed," I told her, trying to keep a grip of myself.

"That's the cop talking," she said softly. "What is the real reason?"

Breaking her stare, I said, "I love Chloe. I don't want to hurt her."

"I love Marc," she said.

"Do you?" I whispered. "Do you really love him?"

"I love you," she said.

To hear those words made me want to wrap her in my arms and never let go. I wanted to lay her down on the bed and undress her. I wanted to know what it would be like to feel Pen naked beneath me as I made love to her over and over. But I couldn't. I loved Chloe, and Pen was right – I was a cop who hunted down Lycanthrope. Being a cop meant something to me. It wasn't just a job anymore. My brother had discovered his vocation early on in his life and I had now found mine. I couldn't uphold the law and track down Lycanthrope if I was prepared to break the law as well.

So with every piece of resolve and strength I could muster, I looked at Pen and said, "I love you, too, but I can't..."

"I understand," she said, turning way.

"Are you happy?" I asked.

With her back facing me, I heard her say, "Yeah, I'm fine. Why shouldn't I be?"

"Dunno, you just seem...well, not yourself. You don't look good, Pen," I told her.

"Gee thanks! You certainly know how to make a girl feel good about herself," she groaned.

"You look like a bag of bones, Pen," I continued. "I'm worried about you."

"I promise you there's nothing wrong," she tried to assure me.

"You would tell me if there was something up, wouldn't you?" I asked.

"I promise," she smiled, then left the room.

We sat on the porch and drank lemonade and talked until the sun had faded. Pen asked if I would ever tell Chloe what I truly was, and I said that I had come close to telling her several times. I'd heard of other relationships between Vampyrus and humans that seemingly worked out okay. These relationships, although frowned upon by the Elders, were allowed. I wanted to ask Pen if she knew the real reason why the mixing between Lycanthrope and Vampyrus was totally forbidden, but I didn't. When we ran out of things to say, we listened to the insects that hummed in the woodland which surrounded Pen's house. When the evening started to cool, Pen disappeared inside. Whilst she was gone, I lit the pipe I had come accustomed to smoking. Most of my colleagues laughed at me, saying that it was an old man's habit, but I enjoyed the warm sensation that the smoke gave in the back of my throat. It relaxed me somehow and took the edge off my cravings for the red stuff.

Pen reappeared with a couple of blankets and a tray, which was loaded with bottles of Coke and popcorn.

"Sorry it's not Bree seeds and Inferno Berry Juice," she smiled, setting the tray down. I took one of the blankets and tossed it around my shoulders to block out the chill. I reached into the huge bowl of popcorn and it was warm to the touch. I chucked a handful into my mouth.

"It's been a long time since we did anything like this together," Pen said, taking her seat again.

"It must be about nine or ten years!"

"That long, huh?"

"Who would have thought, all those years ago that you would have turned out owning a cafe from Oz and me a cop," I mused.

"Yeah, you a cop...amazing," she said with a big smirk on her face.

"What do you mean by that?"

Pen clutched her face in her hands and in a scared little voice, she cried, "Jim Murphy, the great werewolf hunter!"

"Oh my, what big claws you have," I laughed, taking a handful of popcorn from the bowl and throwing it all over her.

We spent the rest of the evening chucking popcorn at one another and singing songs from those magical moving pictures, *The Wizard of Oz*.

Over that weekend I hadn't seen Marc once. He was up and gone before I rose in the morning and didn't come home until I had gone to bed. When I broached this subject with Pen, she told me that Marc had been working long hours at the café, as Easter was one of their busiest times with tourists. I lied and told Pen it would have been nice to have caught up with Marc before I left. Pen finally relented and on my last morning with her, we drove down to 'The Ooze Bar.'

The bar hadn't opened yet for the day, and when we walked in, Annie was cleaning behind the bar and the jukebox was playing quietly in the corner.

"Hello again," I said.

"Hi, Jim. How are you?" she beamed. This was the first time I had seen her without the lion's make-up and she had an impish little face that was unusually pretty.

"I'm okay," I said.

"Where's Marc?" Pen asked her.

"He's down in the basement changing over the barrels," Annie explained.

"No I'm not, I'm here," a voice said from behind us.

We all turned to find Marc standing in the doorway that led down to the basement.

"Hi!" I called out to him.

"Hello, Jim," he said briskly. Then, turning to look at Pen, he added, "Can I have a word in private?" He then turned and disappeared back down the stairs and into the basement.

Pen looked at Annie and me and said, "Sorry about this, I'll be back in a minute."

I watched Pen disappear, then, said to Annie, "I'd sure like to know what fitness program Pen's been keeping to. I could sure do with losing some weight like her."

Annie eyed me suspiciously, then said in a hushed tone, "Hasn't Pen told you?"

"Told me what?" I asked.

"Nothing. It doesn't matter," she sighed as if she'd said something she really shouldn't have.

I reached across the bar and took hold of her hand. "Look, if there's something wrong with Pen, I want to know!"

"Look, I can't...It's none of my business. I shouldn't have said anything." Annie tried to remove her hand from mine but I tightened my grip so she couldn't get away.

"Look, sweetheart, as far as I understand it, Pen's been pretty good to you..." I started.

"I can't, Jim. I'm scared!" Annie had a desperate, almost haunted look in her young eyes.

"Scared of what?" I persisted.

Before she had a chance to say anything more, we could hear footfalls on the basement staircase. Annie wrenched her hand free and went back to cleaning behind the bar. I looked in the direction of the door and saw Pen appear at the top of the stairs alone. She looked pale and shaken.

"Pen, are you okay?" I asked.

"Yeah, I just don't feel too good." She made her way to the exit.

I started to follow, when Annie said, "See ya around, Jim."

I turned to face her and she had her hand outstretched towards me. I stepped towards her and shook her hand. She pulled me close as if to kiss my cheek.

"Call me," she whispered in my ear.

I pulled away, letting go of her hand. As I walked towards the door and the street outside, I opened my hand and found a small piece of paper. I unfolded it to find Annie had scribbled her phone number across it.

What was going on? I wondered, placing the piece of paper into my pocket.

Chapter Fourteen

Murphy

All the way from 'The Ooze Bar' until I dropped Pen back at her house, I tried to find out from her what had happened down in the basement. Pen kept persisting that nothing had happened and she had started to feel ill, that was all. Although I didn't believe her, I didn't push the issue and I never mentioned to her about the scrap of paper Annie had given to me.

I collected my bags and placed them in the boot of my car.

"Pen, I don't know what's going on down here, maybe one day you'll tell me. If you need anything, you know how to get in touch." I pulled her close and kissed her gently on the cheek. Pen didn't say a word. She just stood there looking tired and frail.

I climbed into my car and drove away with a feeling of dread gnawing away at my insides.

On my return home, I didn't hesitate in calling Annie. The phone rang at her end several times, then there was a click on the line, followed by the sound of her voice.

"Hello?"

"Hi, Annie, it's Jim," I said.

"Hiya, Jim," she came back hesitantly.

"Is this a good time for you, or do you..." I started.

"No, it's okay, I've just got Katie off to sleep."

"So what's going on with Pen?" I asked her.

There was a short silence before she said anything. "If I

tell you, Jim, you've got to promise me you won't say anything to Pen. If you let her know I've spoken to you then Marc might find out...and that would mean trouble...real trouble."

"What do you mean?"

"Promise me, Jim. I have Katie to think of. I don't want any trouble. I'm scared," she whispered.

"Scared of what?"

"Promise me!" she demanded.

"Okay. Okay. I promise I won't let on that we've spoken. Now what's going on?" I insisted.

"It's Marc...he's a bully...no it's more than that...he's violent towards Pen."

"What do you mean by violent?" I questioned, those interrogation skills coming to the fore.

"He beats Pen. You know...punches her...kicks her...he's even thrown Pen down the stairs," she said, her voice sounding shaky.

I could feel my stomach begin to twist into angry knots inside me. "How do you know this?"

"Pen has turned up at my house in the early hours of the morning, scared and shaking. I've seen the bruises all over her body. There have been scratches and cuts, too. She's hidden here with me for days on end, trying to keep out of Marc's way."

"Pen's got to get rid of him...throw him out...sack him...whatever it takes," I said, fighting to keep my anger in check.

"Pen's tried, Jim, but she's frightened of Marc and his brother."

"Pen mentioned that Marc had a brother...Steve I think she said his name was. He works as a chef at the bar," I said into the phone.

"Steve's no chef. They're criminals, both of them. Marc's

giving his brother money every week out of the cash register, but he's not actually doing any work. They are running up credit card bills in Pen's name. They're taking huge amounts of money out of the accounts, bills aren't being paid, and they're running the café into the ground. The two of them are ripping Pen off and when she tries to do anything, they hurt her."

"Why hasn't Pen told me any of this?" I asked, shocked and angry at what I had learnt.

"Marc hates you. I think it's because you're a cop. He's also really paranoid and jealous of you," Annie explained, and I knew why Marc hated me – I was a Vampyrus and cop who hunted his kind down. "Pen told me that Marc accuses her of having sex with you."

"What!" I couldn't believe what I was hearing. "Pen and I love each other like a brother and sister would. We could never mix...I mean, be anything more than that."

"Marc has told Pen that if she so much as says anything to you about what's going on then they'll kill her," Annie said, and I could hear her voice waver.

"But that's just a threat. They wouldn't really kill Pen," but I didn't really believe that – although I knew it was unlikely a Lycanthrope would kill another. They would usually get someone else to do their dirty work. I just had to believe that was true.

"Wanna bet? They've both been to jail. Steve's been in jail for various thefts and robberies, and Marc's been down for violence and fraud. These two guys are assholes, Jim," Annie said.

I was seething and I had every intention of getting back into my car and driving straight back there and arresting the two of them myself.

"Look, Annie, when I promised I wouldn't say anything, I didn't realize it would be something as serious as this. I don't think I can keep what you have told me a secret," I told her.

"You promised, Jim!" she cried, and I could hear the fear in her voice. "Please, I beg you! Don't say anything. If they find out it was me…God knows what they would do. I live here on my own with Katie…I don't want any trouble." She began to sob.

"Okay, okay. You have my word, but I'm gonna have to think about this. Maybe I could contact the local police down there and let them know what's going on," I said, desperately racking my own brains to find a way in which I could help Pen.

"Pen doesn't want the cops getting involved. She said they wouldn't understand," Annie said. I knew why Pen thought that – she knew that if the Vampyrus cops got a whiff of what was going on, they would come quickly and in numbers to Pen's café and sort out the problems there in their own unique way. That could cause problems for Pen if she were trying to make a life for herself amongst the humans.

"Okay, I promise I won't go to the local cops, but I need to do something and I promise whatever I decide upon, no one will ever know that it was you who told me, Annie," I whispered into the phone.

Before we said goodbye, Annie promised that she would be there for Pen and that she could always stay with her if she needed to do so. I was grateful to her for looking after Pen for me. Annie also said she would secretly keep me informed of what was going on down there.

When Chloe got home that night, she immediately knew I was upset, as I was pacing back and forth across the living room floor. While she got changed out of her uniform, I made us both supper. As I sat and watched her fork the hash brown casserole into her mouth, I told her about my trip to see Pen and what I had found out from Annie.

Chloe's first reaction was to tell me I had to do something about it. I told her I needed to think about what I was going to do. She looked curiously at me, as she didn't truly understand the dilemma I faced. How I wished I could tell her the truth about what Pen and me really were – where we'd really come from.

As we lay next to each other in bed that night, I listened to the soft sound of Chloe's breathing. I went over and over in my head what Annie had told me. I swung from deep anger towards Marc and his brother to sadness and fear for Pen. As I rolled onto my side and closed my eyes, I could picture Pen and me sitting together in those vast caves, the light from those moving magical pictures flickering in our young eyes. Everything had seemed so much simpler back then.

Over the next few days I agonised over what I should do to help Pen. I thought about calling her, but I knew once I heard her voice, I wouldn't be able to conceal my feelings and I would have to tell Pen that I knew. Therefore, I didn't want to speak to her until I had formulated a plan. A plan that would reassure her and make her feel safe in the knowledge I knew what was going on, and a way to rescue her.

Almost every one of my waking hours and most of my dreams were spent going over and over different ways of helping Pen. I thought about telling my Inspector, but he would only want to know how I had become so close to a Lycanthrope. He would ask why I cared for Pen – a wolf – so much. He might suspect something that wasn't really there – or perhaps it was? Every time the phone rang, I leapt upon it, wondering if it was Annie with more news about Pen, as I hadn't heard anything more from her since our last phone call.

Then on the fourth day after that call with Annie, I did receive some news. It didn't come in the form of a phone call as

I was expecting, but by letter. I'd discovered the envelope in the mailbox as I left home for work that morning. As I was climbing into my car, I pulled the envelope open to read the shortest letter I had ever received. It read: *Pen's gone missing!*

Chapter Fifteen

Murphy

Whoever had written the note, I didn't recognise their handwriting. It had been scribbled in black ink. As I turned it over and over in my hands and re-read those three frightening words, I realized that Annie had been true to her word and had contacted me as promised. I understood the reason why she wanted to do this anonymously, so she didn't appear to be involved.

I contacted my work and lied to my Inspector. I told him my mother had taken a turn for the worse, and I had to go back into The Hollows to be with her. He gave me three days special leave. I threw some clothes into a bag and packed my cuffs and handgun. Before I left, I held Chloe tight and kissed her goodbye. I felt apprehensive, anxious, but most of all, scared for Pen.

I drove all day, stopping only briefly when I needed to fill the car up with petrol and top myself up with sweet black coffee. I reached Pen's hometown just after dark and rented a room at the local hotel. Without even freshening up or stopping for food, I drove straight to Pen's. I pulled up the short path and left the car parked next to an old truck that stood by the dense crop of trees which surrounded the side and rear of the house. I walked casually around the truck, which I had not seen before. I made my way up onto the porch and knocked on the door. After several moments, the door was slowly opened.

"Yep?" said the tall, stocky male who greeted me.

"I'd like to see Pen," I said in a flat, dry tone.

"She's not here." The man eyed me suspiciously and

stepped out onto the porch and pulled the door shut so I couldn't see past him and into the house.

"I'll wait then," I said, moving towards the front door. The man stepped between me and the door, barring my entry.

"Who are ya?" he asked.

"I'm Jim Murphy, a friend of Pen's. Who are you?" I asked, looking him up and down.

"I'm Steve, Marc's brother."

"The chef!" I said dryly.

Steve stood about six-foot-two with lank brown hair, it could have been blond but it was so greasy it was hard to tell. His two front teeth were missing and his tongue slid wetly between them as he spoke. He had about four days' worth of beard covering his chin and his eyes were yellow and sore-looking, as if he had just got up after a night of heavy drinking.

"Look, what do ya want?" he questioned irritably as if he had a thousand better things he could be doing.

"I've told you, I *want* to see Pen," I said.

"And I've told ya, she *ain't* here!" he said, his wet tongue slipping between the gap in his front teeth.

"When will she back?" I persisted.

"Dunno," he shrugged. "Look, go home. I reckon she'll call ya when she can." Steve then stepped back inside Pen's home and briskly closed the door.

I stepped back off the porch and looked up at the windows for any sign of life. Maybe they had Pen held prisoner up there while they fleeced her and her business of any remaining cash. My imagination was running wild, stoked up by not knowing where Pen was or what had happened to her. Whatever was going on, I knew that Marc and his brother had something to do with it.

I went back to my car, and as I pulled away, I looked back at the house and caught Steve peering around the edge of the curtain at me.

I drove into town and pulled up outside 'The Ooze Bar.' I could see it was slowly building up with customers for the evening and I could hear the dull *beat-beat* of music seeping from within.

I stepped into the bar and immediately, as if she had been expecting me, Annie looked up from the customer she was serving and looked straight at me. I could see a look of relief slip across her face, but her eyes looked wide and scared. At the end of the bar I could see Marc. I moved towards him, and when I was only a few feet away, he looked up at me.

"Where's Pen?" I asked him.

"She's gone away," he said right back.

"Where?"

"I don't know," Marc said, shrugging his shoulders nonchalantly.

"Look I haven't come down here to be screwed around. Where's Pen?" I demanded.

"Listen, you're not on duty now. So don't come down here throwing your weight around," he said, climbing off the barstool and standing like a wall in front of me. "Pen hasn't been feeling well lately, so she's taken a break, you know, gone away to relax."

"She would've called me," I said.

"Maybe she's having so much fun she has forgotten," Marc said slyly, an obnoxious grin spreading across his face.

"I doubt it," I told him.

"Can't poor Pen do anything without you? What are you, her guardian angel?" he said in a deeply cutting tone.

I stepped closer towards him, narrowing the gap between us to mere inches. Then leaning in close so I couldn't be heard by anyone other than him, I said, "Listen, you know and I know something's not right here. You might have been able to intimidate Pen with the help of your brothers, but to me you're nothing but werewolf shit." I noticed just a slight flicker of light in his eyes.

"Why don't you go home? When Pen puts in an appearance, I'm sure you'll be the first to know," he smiled.

"I'm not going anywhere 'til I find out what's happened to my friend," I warned him, looking hard into his fiery eyes. I wanted him to be under no illusion that I wouldn't go away until I had discovered what had happened to Pen.

"Please yourself," he said, turning away and stepping behind the bar.

I watched him saunter away from me, and as he did, I noticed the door leading down to the basement. It was slightly ajar and I could only see darkness behind. I looked away, and as I did, I thought I saw movement in that opening. I looked back again but whatever it was had gone. I slowly walked towards the door and instinctively touched my gun that sat strapped to my side, hidden under my jacket. I put my arm out to push the door further open, when Marc was suddenly in front of me, blocking my view.

"That's private down there. Staff only I'm afraid," he said.

I ignored him and made a move towards the door leading down into the darkness. Within an instant, Marc had placed his arm across the doorway, barring my entry.

"Do you have a search warrant, *officer*?" he asked smugly.

I stood exactly where I was for another moment, not taking my eyes off his. I then stepped away from him.

"I'm coming to get you!" I said smiling at him. "Just like all the other stinking wolves I've hunted down."

Then, I turned my back on him and walked towards the exit. As I did, I snatched a sideways glance at Annie. Our eyes met momentarily and then we both looked away.

Chapter Sixteen

Murphy

I pulled into the car park of the local store and killed the engine. There was a phone box, so climbing from my car, I headed towards it. Taking some coins from my pocket, I called my Inspector. I didn't want to, but I needed some help. Like me, he was a Vampyrus and had dedicated his life to hunting down and bringing to justice those Lycanthrope who had given in to their curse. He would know I'd lied to him about needing to visit my sick mother, and he could kick me off the team for it, but what else could I do? I needed some help – advice – if I was going to help my friend.

I dropped the coins into the slot and punched my Inspector's office number into the keypad. There was a clicking sound, followed by a dial tone.

"Inspector Rom, Special Ops Department," the voice said down the phone. I could picture his bald head gleaming beneath the fluorescent lights in his office.

"Hello, sir," I said, still not knowing exactly what I was going to say to him. "It's Jim Murphy."

"Murphy, what can I do for you?" he asked. "How's your sick mother?"

"Huh, she's okay," I started. "Look, I was wondering if..."

"Spit it out, Constable," Rom said sharply. "I'm giving a briefing in a minute or two to the team."

I took a deep breath, which Rom must have heard at the other end of the line as he said, "Are you in some kinda trouble, boy?"

"I guess," I said.

"Oh, shit," Rom groaned. "How deep?"

"It's not really me, it's a friend..." I started.

"A girl?" Rom sighed.

"Yes, but it's not what you're thinking," I said. "It's worse."

"Is this girl married?" Rom barked.

"No..." I took another deep breath. "She's a Lycanthrope."

There was a long, drawn-out silence from the other end of the line. It was so long and deep that I wondered if Rom hadn't slammed down the phone on me.

"A Lycanthrope?" he suddenly breathed down the line. "Are you out of your fucking mind?"

"She's just a friend," I told him again. "Nothing like that has gone on. I've known her since we were just kids. It's her who's in trouble."

"She's a Lycanthrope, Murphy," Rom hissed. "She ain't your problem."

"She's my friend and I think she has been murdered," I said.

There was another long pause. Then suddenly, "Murdered by who?"

"A couple of Lycanthrope," I explained.

"Then that's not my problem or *yours*," Rom said. "Now get your arse back to work and I'll speak to you then."

"I can't come back – not yet," I told him. "Not until I've found out what has happened to my friend."

"You don't make friends with wolves," he reminded me. "We're like cats and dogs. We don't *mix*. Now grow up and get your sorry arse back..."

"I'm not coming back," I said, drawing another deep breath and feeling sick inside. "Not until I've found out what has happened to her."

Another long silence.

"What makes you think she has been murdered?" he finally said.

"Pen...that's her name...has been living with this guy, you see..." I began to tell him. I explained about the 'Ooze Bar', Marc, and his brother. Rom asked for their surname and I got the feeling that he was writing down what I was telling him. Did this mean he was going to help? I couldn't be sure. I explained how Marc had been beating Pen and stealing money from her business.

When I'd finished, Rom spoke again. "Listen, Murphy, these people...*wolves*, they don't live like us," he warned me in an almost fatherly tone. "Nothing good will come of this. As far as you know, they haven't killed no human, so if I were you, I'd leave them to get on with it."

"I can't," I whispered. "Pen is my friend. I can't just walk away."

Realising he wasn't going to change my mind, he sighed deeply and said, "You're a good cop, Murphy. I had high hopes for you. Why you've gone and got yourself mixed up with a Lycanthrope beats the shit out of me."

"She's my friend," was all I could say.

"I know I'm going to regret this," he sighed. "I'll do some digging on this Marc Johnson and his brother on my end and see what I come up with. Give me some information on this *friend* of yours."

I gave Rom Pen's description, car registration number, address, and anything else I could think of. I then thanked him.

"Don't thank me," he said. "When you get back, me and you are going to have a serious talk about your future on the Force. Now, for Christ's sake, sit tight and don't get involved."

I gave Rom the number of the hotel I was staying at and thanked him again.

"If it wasn't the fact that you were a Vampyrus and a

110

cop, I'd come down there and kill this freaking wolf, Pen, myself!" He hung up the phone.

Chapter Seventeen

Murphy

Despite Rom's warning not to get involved, I drove back across town, which was now mostly quiet and deserted. It was just short of midnight and I guessed that 'The Ooze bar' would be closing soon. I parked just up the street and slid down into my seat and waited for Annie to leave the bar for the night. It was just a waiting game now. It was a game that I had played countless times before, back home while at work.

By 1:30 a.m. there had still been no sign of Annie. I twisted in my seat and stretched. Maybe I had missed her already? Maybe she finished earlier, before I had even arrived? I had decided to give her another half an hour, when I saw her step out of 'The Ooze Bar' and into the night.

I started the engine and crawled slowly up the road some distance behind her. I waited until she had walked a couple of streets and was a safe distance from the bar, when I drew up alongside her and wound down my window.

"Hey, Annie!"

She quickened her pace and didn't turn to look at me or the car.

"Hey, Annie, it's me, Jim!"

On realising who it was, she slowed slightly and looked through the open window at me.

"Go away!" she whispered and flashed a quick glance behind her.

"Get in," I said.

"No! Go away," she pleaded.

"I just wanted to say thanks for the note."

"What note? I never sent any note," she said, looking

straight ahead.

"Okay, okay...I never got any note," I played along. I continued to crawl along beside her as she began to quicken her step.

"How long has Pen been missing?"

"About four days. Now please, just leave me alone!" she said without even turning to look at me.

"You don't have to be scared, Annie, I can protect you. Just tell me what you know," I said.

"I won't need protecting if you just go away!" she whispered.

"Why are you so scared, Annie?"

"Because I feel that something very bad has happened...I think something *bad* has happened to Pen." This time she did glance sideways at me and I could see the fear in her eyes.

"Like what?" I persisted.

"I don't know!"

"What's in the basement?" I pressed.

"Nothing, I think...please, Jim, please leave me alone," she said.

I could sense her fear and didn't want to alienate her completely. I hoped that she could maybe be a future source of information – so I let her be.

"Okay, Annie, I'm sorry. Look I'm staying at the local hotel. I'm in room 219 for the next two days. If you need anything or hear anything, just let me know."

Annie took a sharp right turn and hastily disappeared down another street. I wound up my window and drove straight on – losing Annie from my sight.

Chapter Eighteen

Murphy

I was woken to the sound of the telephone ringing. I reached for the phone with my eyes still closed, and knocked it onto the floor of my hotel room. I wriggled from beneath my blankets, dangled over the side of the bed, and picked up the receiver.

"Hello," I said, stifling a yawn.

"Rise and shine, Murphy," Rom snapped down the line at me. Even half asleep, I could picture his pinched-looking face and sharp, keen probing eyes. Not the thing I wanted to see first thing in the morning.

"Hello, sir," I said, sitting up in bed.

"I've got some news for you," he said. "I ran the Johnson boys' names through the system. They're nothing but scum by the looks of it. The whole family is rotten through and through. There ain't a decent wolf amongst 'erm."

"You ever had dealings with them before?" I asked, rubbing sleep from my eyes with my free hand. My mouth tasted like I'd been eating road kill.

"All their lives they've been in and out of jail...and you say your friend...this Pen, has been living with one of 'erm?" he said.

"Yes, the one called Marc," I reminded him.

"Well, I got someone who owed me a few favours to do some checking on her, too," Rom told me. "Her father is doing time down in The Hollows for human child abduction. You really know how to pick your friends."

"Pen hasn't had contact with her father for years," I told him. "He abandoned her. Pen is not like the others."

"Well, I got one of the wardens to visit him down in the cells," Rom started to explain. "Her father didn't want to talk at first, but after my friend yanked on his bollocks for a minute or two, he couldn't wait to start talking. Apparently, your friend Pen has been promised to this Marc Johnson."

"What does that mean exactly?" I asked Rom, now feeling fully awake.

"Her father lost her in a card game some years ago..." Rom started.

"A card game!" I spat.

"He was playing cards and losing bad," Rom said. "He had nothing left in the pot to gamble with so he offered up his young daughter. He lost and your friend Pen was then promised to Johnson's eldest son, Marc, when she came of age."

"Those fucking animals," I breathed angrily down the phone.

"Tell me something I don't already know," Rom said. "Don't you see now? These wolves don't live like us. They're scum. Don't get involved in this, Murphy. It's not your problem. However much it disgusts us, these wolves made a deal years ago for Pen and they are keeping to it. Just come home."

"I can't, not until I know Pen is safe," I breathed down the phone.

"She is alive," he suddenly said.

"How do you know?" I asked, jumping from the bed, and reaching for my clothes with my free hand.

"Her car registration popped up at a local ANPR system just a few days ago," Rom said.

"Where?" I snapped.

"On Bleachers Road," he said.

"I know it," I breathed. "It's the main road which heads out of town."

"Then that's your answer," Rom sighed. "Your friend has

hit the road. Decided to do a runner from this guy she's been promised to. Just come home, son. You never know; she might show up here."

To hear that Pen's car had been pinged by the local Automatic Number Plate Recognition cameras raised my hopes that she was safe and well.

"Are you still there, Murphy?" Rom asked, cutting into the silence.

"Huh?" I said thoughtfully. "Yeah, I'm still here."

"There's nothing you can do to help," Rom said. "Don't get yourself in wolf issues – not this kind anyhow."

"But..." I started.

"No *buts*, Murphy," Rom barked, any understanding that he might have felt for me now gone. "Get your arse back home. I'll see you in my office at nine tomorrow morning!"

The phone *clicked* as he cut the line dead.

I placed the phone back on the stand beside the bed. Was Pen really alive and well? I wondered. I hoped so. Maybe she was in hiding somewhere? Perhaps she had rented a room? But what I couldn't understand was – why hadn't she contacted me?

With these thoughts clawing away at me, I took a shower and got dressed. I slipped my handcuffs through the loop on my belt, holstered my gun, threw on my jacket, and headed for the door. It was then that I saw the envelope lying on the floor. I picked it up and turned it over in my hands. On the front somebody had scribbled '*Jim*'. I yanked open my hotel door; there was no one there. I tore open the envelope and read what was written on the folded piece of paper inside:

Check out Dorothy's ruby slippers!

I recognised the handwriting as that of the previous

letter writer. Why can't Annie just talk to me, instead of posting these cryptic messages? I wondered. But then again, if she felt secure in communicating with me in this way, it was okay with me. At least somebody was prepared to help me find out what had happened to Pen.

Check out Dorothy's ruby slippers! But what does it mean? I wondered. I placed the piece of paper back into the envelope and tucked it into my jacket pocket.

I remembered the night Pen and I had spent in The Hollows watching the magical moving pictures, *The Wizard of Oz*, together. I could clearly see Dorothy standing there, beautiful and innocent, clicking the heels of her ruby slippers together and saying over and over, *'There's no place like home! There's no place like home!'*

Maybe that was it! Perhaps that was what the message alluded to – Pen had gone home? Maybe she had had enough of Marc and his brother and her ailing bar and had just gone back to her world beyond the Fountain of Souls.

No, not likely, I pondered. Pen had told me of her reluctance to ever go home again. Perhaps she had found some other place to live? But it always came back to the same question: *If Pen had done any of these things, why hadn't she contacted me?*

"Think, Jim, think," I said out loud.

Rom had said that I had to be in the office by 9 a.m. tomorrow morning, so that gave me less than twenty-four hours to find out what had happened to Pen. Rom seemed to believe that Pen was alive because her car had been...

I picked up the phone again and dialled his number.

"Rom," he said irritably.

"It's Mur..." I started.

"This had better be good!" he snapped.

"You said that Pen's car had been picked up on that

ANPR camera, I said. "But that doesn't mean she was driving it."

"Jesus-wept," Rom groaned. "Stop chasing ghosts and get your arse back..."

"Can you get someone to pull the images?" I asked, my heart thumping. I knew I had already pushed my luck with Rom.

"Listen to me!" Rom roared, and I had to pull the phone away from my ear, he bellowed so loud. "I've got better things to do than go wasting my time chasing wolves..."

"But I believe Pen has been murdered," I said. "Please help me and I promise as soon as I get back I'll happily give you my badge and leave the Force. I just need to know that my friend is..."

"She's a wolf!" he cut in.

"But she's not like the others," I insisted. "I thought the Vampyrus were meant to help those wolves who wanted to break free of their curse..."

"And we are," Rom barked. "But I think you're too close to this wolf. I believe your judgment is clouded."

"What's so wrong about wanting to help a friend?"

"She's a wolf!" he almost screamed.

"So she doesn't deserve our protection, then?" I tried to reason.

There was a silence. I waited for his response to come.

"You don't leave that hotel room until I call you back," he said finally, then hung up the phone.

Loosening my jacket, I lay back on my unmade bed. I crossed my legs at the ankles and laced my fingers behind me head. My mind went back to the note which Annie had snuck beneath the door for me. Then sitting bolt upright, I shouted, "Of course! Dorothy's ruby slippers! The ruby slippers in the display case in Pen's bedroom!"

That was the answer. That was what Annie had been guiding me to in her letter. But having the answer only perplexed me further. How would those ruby slippers help me find Pen? What did they have to do with her disappearance? And the biggest question of all – how was I going to get to those ruby slippers with Marc and Steve living at Pen's house?

Chapter Nineteen

Murphy

I popped the end of my pipe between my lips, lit it, and inhaled deeply.

When was I gonna get a half-decent break? I asked myself. I was running around in circles. My best friend had suddenly vanished, or worse, there were two criminals encamped in her house, I've got a single mum who's too scared to even talk to me but has a passion for sending me cryptic messages that the FBI would have difficulty in cracking, and my Inspector wants to sack me!

As I contemplated my next move, I puffed on my pipe and squirted jets of smoke out through my nostrils. I still had the ruby slipper mystery to solve...whatever that had to do with anything, I did not know. All I could do was wait for Rom to get back to me. Perhaps he was right and Pen had driven off, so desperate to escape Marc and his brother that she didn't have the chance to contact me. I couldn't do anything for sure until I had some kind of proof that Pen had been hurt, or worse. I spent the day pacing back and forth across my hotel room. I didn't want to go out for food just in case I missed Rom's telephone call, so I ordered some to my room.

I chewed the ham and cheese sandwich without even tasting it. I flicked through the TV channels, my eyes not even focusing what played across the screen. The hours ticked slowly by – dragging out like a long shadow. Then, as the afternoon slipped into early evening, the phone rang. I snatched the receiver from its cradle and placed it against my ear.

"Murphy?" Rom said.

"Have you found anything?" I asked.

"Okay, this still doesn't mean anything..." he started.

"What doesn't?" I cut in.

"I've seen the picture the ANPR camera snapped and it wasn't..."

"Who was driving the car?" I demanded.

"The picture isn't great, but the person behind the wheel is definitely male. Longish, dark hair..." he started to explain.

"Marc," I breathed over him.

"We don't know that for sure," Rom tried to reason. "And even if it was – so what does that prove? Perhaps he borrowed your friend's car."

"Not likely," I said. Then thinking of the note which had been placed under my door, I added, "I have just one more lead I want to follow up."

"No!" Rom barked. "You get your arse back here right..."

I hung up the phone before he'd had a chance to finish.

I was now convinced that some harm had come to Pen at the hands of Marc and his brother, Steve. I knew the time I would spend trying to convince Rom that Pen was in danger would be wasted, and time was something I feared I didn't have a lot of. My plan wasn't to storm over to Pen's and confront Marc straight away – no, I needed to get into the house unbeknown to him and Steve, and take a look at those ruby slippers. They must bear some significance on Pen's disappearance; otherwise Annie wouldn't have pointed me in their direction. The more evidence I had confirming Pen had been a victim of foul play, the more chance I had of convincing Rom to launch an investigation into her disappearance.

I checked my weapon, holstered it beneath my jacket along with my cuffs, and left my hotel room. It was fully dark now, and cold. A fine drizzle was in the air, and by the time I had reached my car, my hair and jacket were wet. I started the engine and swung out of the car park.

When I got near to Pen's house, I pulled off the road and parked my car up a little dirt track about a mile away and took a torch from the boot of the car. I made my way through the wooded area, which stood tall and overgrown on either side of the dirt track, and set off in the direction of Pen's house. I walked for about twenty minutes through the trees until I could see Pen's house in the clearing ahead. I positioned myself so I could see who was coming and if anyone was leaving. Hunkering down, I made myself small between the trunks of the trees. I could see the old blue truck which had been parked there the day before. I figured at least Steve was at home if not Marc, as well.

Glancing down at my watch and it was just short of 8 p.m. I settled against the tree in the darkness and waited. At just gone half past eight, Pen's front door was swung open and Steve appeared on the porch. He stood momentarily and picked the seat of his pants from the crack in his arse. If that wasn't bad enough, he stuffed a finger up his nostril and began having a good root around. After digging away for several seconds, he pulled his finger out and studied the snot he had retrieved. After inspecting it for a moment or two, he popped it into his mouth.

"C'mon!" he yelled back into the house.

"You go ahead, I'll catch up with you later," shouted Marc from inside.

Steve then swung the front door closed, farted, sighed, and then got into the truck and drove off.

"Filthy animal," I grumbled to myself. "One down, one to go!" I sat back against the tree.

I waited patiently for another hour or so before Marc

appeared on the porch. My back had begun to ache and my joints were stiff from sitting in the same position for so long. I could clearly see Marc from my hiding place. He skipped down the steps leading from the porch and went round to the side of the house and out of my view. I then heard the wailing sound of the garage door being pushed up. The noise of a car rumbled into life. Pen's car swung into view, then onto the road. I could see it was being driven by Marc. As he drove off at speed, I got up and my knees made an audible 'cracking' noise. I stood and stretched, waiting just a few more moments until the sound of Pen's car disappeared into the distance.

Once I was sure Marc had gone, I stepped out of the wooded area and went to the rear of Pen's house.

Chapter Twenty

Murphy

Once round the back of the house, I stood on tip toe and rattled the windows in their frames. All of them seemed to be securely fastened. I then went to the back door and pushed and pulled on its handle but without success. I cupped my hands around my eyes and peered through the windowpane in the door and into the kitchen. I couldn't see any movement from inside, and if there had of been anyone else in there, they would have shown themselves while coming to investigate the sound of me yanking on the back door.

I didn't know how much time I had to get in to see what the ruby slippers had to offer. I had to get in then out again without Marc or Steve returning, so I pulled the flashlight from my waistband and smashed the base of it against the window in the back door. I shuddered as the glass splintered noisily and scattered all over the kitchen floor. This hadn't been my first choice of entry. Marc and Steve would have known they'd had an intruder and I doubted it would have taken them very long to work out it had been me. But I needed to get in and out of the house as soon as possible. Once I had been in and done what I needed to do, there was very little they could do about it. Besides, I took a perverse satisfaction in them knowing I wasn't planning on going anywhere until I had discovered what had happened to Pen.

I slid my arm through the broken windowpane and twisted the latch on the other side of the door. I eased it open gently and snuck in, closing the door behind me. I switched on the flashlight and it lit up everything I pointed it at in a warm cone of orange light. I panned it around the room and could see the place was dirty and messy. There were empty beer bottles scattered about the floor and discarded Pizza Hut boxes with half-eaten triangles of pizza lying in grease. I could see ashtrays overflowing with burnt-out cigarette butts perched on the arms of the couch.

Leaving the squalor behind me, I climbed the stairs and went up to Pen's bedroom. I shone the light around the room and could see that her bed was unmade. There were dirty boxer shorts and clothes all over the floor. I crossed the room to where the display cabinet stood and was relieved to see it was still there. The ruby slippers winked on and off at me like a million minute cat eyes in the glare of my torch.

I pulled the glass door open and held the torch between my teeth so I could inspect the slippers. Without touching them, I carried out a visual inspection to see if there was anything obvious about them which I would notice straight away. I screwed up my eyes in the glare of the flashlight, but couldn't see anything abnormal about them. I reached in and removed the left slipper from the display. It came away easily enough and I turned it over and over in my hands. Nothing. I tipped it up, so I could see inside, half expecting to find another note, or a secret key which would lead me to some hidden chamber, and in turn, to Pen. I found nothing. I put the slipper back and picked up the right one. But as I tried to remove this slipper from the cabinet, I felt a little resistance. Gently, I tried to pull the slipper free, but it had been attached to something. I lent as far as I could into the glass structure and peered under the sole of the shoe. It was then I noticed a thin, black wire running out of the heel of the slipper and out through the back of the display cabinet. I placed two fingers inside the slipper and blindly followed the wire which led to the toe. Here I could feel a little piece of hard, square-shaped plastic.

It suddenly dawned on me I had felt something like this before. Something I had handled countless times in the course of my duties as a cop. It was a miniature camera. I removed my fingers and studied the toe of the slipper. Amongst the hundreds of tiny red sequins covering it, I could see the tiny black lens of a camera.

"Pen, Pen, Pen!" I whispered to myself, realising she must have gotten the idea from all of those stories I'd told her about my work.

"But what is it that you want me to see?" I asked, as if she were standing right next to me. "What was it you hoped to catch on camera?"

I placed the slipper back in position and pulled the display case away from the wall. I flashed the light behind it and could see the thin, black wire running out of the back and down beneath the gap between the wall and the edge of the carpet. I hunkered down and followed the wire which led me to a small closet. The wire disappeared around the back so I pulled the closet away from the wall and peered around it. Here I could see a small, square door which was shut flush against the wall. I squeezed between the wall and the closet and prised it open.

With the aid of my torch, I looked inside and saw a DVD recorder with its luminous display panel flashing a sickly green back at me. I could see that the machine was no longer recording, so I pressed the 'Eject' button and a DVD popped out. I removed it and stood up. The fact that the camera was still in place and the DVD had remained untouched, assured me that neither Marc nor Steve were aware of its existence. To say I was curious to find out what was on the disc was an understatement.

"Where would be a safe place to watch it?" I was asking myself when I suddenly heard the front door slam shut downstairs.

I flicked off my torch and stood rigid in the darkness of Pen's bedroom. I tucked the disc inside my jacket and felt the cold metal of my gun. I kept it holstered and crept across the room, hiding behind the open door. I listened intently for any sound of movement from below. It was silent. The only sound was the thumping of my heart in my chest, ears, and throat. It was eerily silent. Then, I heard the sound of broken glass being crunched underfoot.

They're gonna know someone's in here now! I thought to myself as I pictured either Marc or Steve coming across the broken window in the back door.

It went silent again and I strained desperately to try and hear movement. Any sound would do, to give me some idea of how many were in the house and their whereabouts. I eased my gun from its holster and removed the safety catch. Then, suddenly the house was filled with noise. Somebody had started to play music at a deafening level. It was so loud that the thumping bass of the music shook the whole house. I recognised the song to be *Jump Around* by House of Pain. The music pounded like a swollen and blood-filled heart all around me. I immediately knew why the music had been turned on and played at such an ear-piercing level – it was to drown out the sound of them moving around the house in search of me. With the house in total darkness and unable to hear anything, it took away both of my most vital senses.

I crept out of Pen's bedroom and disappeared up the landing with my gun poised.

The song bellowed around the house.

I saw movement out of the corner of my eye and I darted into another bedroom, my breath wheezing shallowly in my chest as I ducked down beside the bed.

The music thumped and pounded, and in the darkness it

had a disorientating effect. I guessed that was the whole idea. I peered again into the darkness on the landing and I thought I caught a fleeting glimpse of someone pass outside the bedroom door at speed.

The song screamed in my ears.

I got up quickly, moving back towards the door. I wanted to keep moving – to try and disorientate *them*.

I went back onto the landing and crouched at the top of the stairs. I felt something behind me in the blackness.

There was a sudden explosion of pain in my ribs. I glanced round to see a boot launching out of the darkness at me. I was kicked viciously in the ribs again, and I sprawled down the stairs, crashing into every step on my way to the bottom. Instinctively, I tried to grab onto something to halt my decent, and accidentally squeezed on the trigger of my handgun. It recoiled violently in my hand as it fired. The darkness flashed with sudden brightness as my gun went off and in that moment of light, I caught a sudden and terrifying glimpse of Marc charging down the stairs towards me. His face looked twisted out of shape. It was like his face had stretched somehow – giving him the appearance of a half wolf and man. His eyes blazed bright yellow.

I landed at the bottom of the stairs and cried out in pain. My lungs felt as if they had been set on fire every time I drew breath. The gun clattered out of my hand and spun away from me and into the darkness.

I staggered to my feet. Marc's fist connected with my chin and I flew backwards, crashing against the wall. I could taste blood in my mouth and my brain swam sickly in my skull from where I had been struck.

It was so loud I didn't even hear Marc approach as he grabbed me by my hair and yanked me off my feet. My eyes had begun to get used to the darkness and I could just make out the shape of his head a few inches from mine. He was so close I could feel his hot breath against my skin and it smelt of stale beer. Sensing his closeness, I rolled my head back and then slammed it forward into his face, my right temple crashing into his nose. I felt warm blood splash across my cheek. I couldn't tell if it was mine or his. I pulled the flashlight from my jacket pocket and shone it widely about the room. Where was my gun?

Marc clattered into me again. Both of us went sprawling across the room. I landed on my back and I could feel him on top of me, crushing my chest under his weight and forcing the air from my lungs. I released my claws and swiped frantically about in the dark. I could hear him woofing and howling above me. Knowing that I had to survive his attack, I thrust my hips upwards sharply, and threw him off me. I rolled onto my stomach. The torch was rolling casually back and forth on the floor, illuminating the area around it and my gun, which was nearby.

Dragging myself forward on my elbows, I headed towards the gun. I was within touching distance of it, when I felt him grab hold of my ankles, yanking me back towards him. I kicked out frantically with my legs, like a wild horse trying desperately to throw its rider.

Boom...Boom...Boom...the music continued all around us like a racing heartbeat.

I managed to work one of my legs free. Twisting slightly, I spun my free leg around, swiping Marc's legs from under him. He crashed to the floor. I reached out and grabbed my gun tightly – so tight I thought my knuckles would burst through my claws. I snatched up my torch with my free hand and shone the light directly into his wolf-like face. I could see it was covered in blood where I had slashed at it with my claws. A flap of skin swung from his right cheek like a strip of liver.

"Shut-the-fuck-up!" I hissed, shooting at the CD player with my gun. The music came to an abrupt stop. The sudden silence was as deafening as the music had been only moments before.

I switched on the light, blinking in its sudden brightness. Marc lay sprawled out on the floor beneath me. His face no longer looked like that of a wolf. Marc's nose looked broken from where I had smashed into it with my forehead. It looked bent, fat and twisted out of shape. Thick black clots of blood ran from both nostrils and into his mouth. I didn't know if I looked as bad as he did, but my head felt as if it had been hit by a speeding train. My bottom lip was fat and swollen out of shape. I suspected I had at least one broken rib.

With a shaking hand, I pointed my gun at his head and said, "Where's Pen?"

"Fuck-you!" he said, spitting a globule of blood up into my face.

It ran off the end of my nose. I wiped it away with the sleeve of my jacket.

"Stand up and turn away from me," I ordered him, my gun aimed straight at his head.

Marc pulled himself slowly to his feet and turned his back to me.

"Put your hands behind your back, lock your fingers together, and lean forward," I ordered.

He did as I said. Quickly, I holstered my gun and placed my handcuffs firmly on his wrists. I took hold of the back of his shirt, shoving him across the living room and down onto the couch.

"What's that?" he asked, as he watched me take the DVD from within my jacket.

"I dunno, let's find out, shall we?" I said with a grim smile.

Chapter Twenty-One

Murphy

I switched on the TV and pushed the DVD into the player beneath it. I took a seat in the chair on the opposite side of the room. From here I could see the TV, but also keep an eye on Marc.

A set of wavy lines rolled across the screen to reveal a window of blackness. It stayed like this for a moment or two before an image flickered onto the screen. It was Pen's bedroom, the viewpoint being the glass cabinet. Pen was lying on top of the bed and she was naked. She looked to be asleep, her hands folded beneath the side of her face like a pillow. Her white-blond hair spilled over her hands and her body looked pale and thin.

Then I saw Marc appear in the shot as he approached Pen, asleep on the bed. He stood and looked down at her, Pen unaware that he was there. I glanced over at him bent forward on the couch and he stared back at me. Then on the film, Marc began to slowly undress, removing his clothes as if they were an extra layer of skin, and letting them slowly slide to the floor. He then knelt on the bed and leant over Pen. Slowly he drew his long fingers along the length of her spine, from the base of her neck all the way down to her buttocks. She stirred. I could see that in the video Marc was aroused. He then rolled Pen onto her back and climbed on top of her. It was then she woke.

"No! No! No!" she screamed.

To hear her terrified voice sent gooseflesh scampering all over my body.

"Shut your fucking mouth!" Marc roared back.

At once she tried to push Marc off and I could see by the

look on her face that she was repulsed by him. Marc gripped hold of her shoulders and pinned her to the bed. Pen screamed out as she fought back, kicking out her legs as she squirmed beneath him.

"Get off me!" Pen screamed, her voice sounding like broken fingernails being drawn across a chalkboard.

"You were promised to me, you little bitch, and I'm gonna take what's mine!" Marc growled as he forced his meaty thigh between Pen's legs.

I snatched another quick look at Marc seated on the other side of the lounge and he looked coldly at what was unfolding before him on the TV. I looked back at the screen. Pen gripped hold of Marc's back as he lay arched over her. Her hands changed from long, slender fingers to huge, white claws. She raked them down his back, his skin splitting open like ripe fruit. Marc slung his head back and howled in pain.

"You fucking whore!" he barked, his bright yellow eyes spinning in their sockets. Pen took this opportunity to wriggle out from beneath him and climb from the bed. With much of her body know covered in a fine white fur, but still looking very much human, she ran around the edge of the bed. Marc shot out one long paw and knocked her flying backwards into the wall. The image shook violently on the screen. Pen howled in pain. Marc sprang from the bed. He too was now covered in fur, which was thick and dark.

"You were promised to me!" he woofed, as he loomed over Pen.

She lay at his feet, her legs drawn up to protect herself and her dignity.

"I'm not yours!" she screamed at him, her eyes wide and bright. "I don't love you, I love another."

Marc recoiled as if slapped by an invisible hand. "Say his name! Say his name!" Marc roared, the long lengths of hair swinging wildly from the sides of his face and beneath his chin. His giant paws swung by his fur-covered thighs.

"I love Jim Murphy and I always have!" Pen screeched at him. "It's him that I want – not you!"

"You want a filthy Vampyrus cop!" Marc howled in disgust. "You want to fuck a flea-infested bat?"

"I love him!" Pen screamed, waving her claws out before her as if to warn him off. To hear her scream those words crushed me. For I knew that I was in love with her, too – always had been, even though I had found love with another – Chloe. What caused me more pain than anything was the fact that I hadn't been around to protect Pen.

Then Marc was on her, his arms and legs nothing more than a blur as he kicked and clawed at her. Jets of blood and chunks of her white fur splattered the floor, bed, and walls. Again, I looked over at Marc and he stared at me with indifference. I stared blankly back at the TV screen, feeling numb and sick. Hot bile flushed into my mouth, but it didn't sting as much as the tears, which streamed silently down my face. Pen stopped flailing her arms and legs about, as Marc placed his giant claws about her throat and squeezed. Pen's eyes bulged hard and round in their sockets, her tongue jerking up and down at the corner of her mouth. Then she fell still.

I looked over at Marc and suddenly he looked ill. I doubted that he looked like this through remorse, but more likely because his crime had been caught on camera. I couldn't hold it back any longer. I suddenly brought up the contents of my stomach. Hot sick shot from my mouth and squirted out of my nose and splattered over the floor at my feet. I couldn't believe – understand – how I had just watched the brutal murder of the person I loved.

On the TV screen, Marc got off Pen. He stood panting like a tired dog, his tongue lolling from the corner of his mouth.

He then bent forward, and snatching up Pen's lifeless body as if she was nothing more than a sack full of rubbish, he carried her from the room.

I wiped the sick from my lips with the back of my hand, pulled out my gun, and crossed the room. I stood before Marc and placed the end of the gun against his forehead.

"Go on then, shoot me," he said without a note of fear in his voice. *"Go on! Fucking shoot me!"* he screamed.

I knew that I couldn't – not now – not without a trial before the Elders. However much I wanted Marc dead – he had to be tried. That was what I had signed up for by carrying a police badge. If I killed him now, I became him. I became no better than a Lycanthrope. That's why the Vampyrus were different – we lived by rules. I wasn't a mindless killer.

I looked into his eyes, and then holstered my weapon.

"No...I'm better than you," I said coldly and dragged him to his feet.

Chapter Twenty-Two

Murphy

I pushed Marc down the porch steps and onto the drive. I followed close behind him. I felt numb and bewildered by what I had just seen. I still hadn't fully comprehended that Pen was dead.

I forced Marc towards the treeline and turned on my torch as we made our way towards the wooded area. Then, suddenly there seemed little need for my torch. We were caught in the glare of the headlights of Steve's truck as he drove it onto the driveway. Seeing this, Marc looked up and began to howl at his brother.

"Steve, he's got me! He knows everything! Steve!"

I grabbed hold of Marc, his hands still cuffed behind his back, and forced him off the drive and in amongst the trees.

"Steve! Steve! Help me, Steve!" Marc continued to bark.

"Shut the fuck up!" I hissed, pushing and shoving him ahead of me. Again, I flipped off the torch and for the second time that night, I was staggering around blindly in the dark. I tried to head in a straight line, in the direction I had left my car. I looked back and could see torchlight bobbing about behind us.

"Marc! Where are you, Marc?" Steve cried.

"Over here! I'm over here!" Marc shouted back into the darkness.

I glanced over my shoulder and could see Steve's torchlight heading towards us at speed.

"I said, shut the fuck up!" I hissed at Marc again.

He ignored me and howled again, *"Steve! Over here,*

Steve!"

Steve was very close now, so I forced Marc down into the undergrowth. I lay on top of him, and in the dark I felt for his mouth with my hand. Once I had located it, I forced the barrel of my gun between his teeth. I put my cheek next to his and whispered into his ear.

"You don't hear too well. One more word out of you...so much as a murmur, and you won't believe what happens next. I'll execute you and your fucking brother. Do I make myself clear?"

Marc nodded very slowly, not out of obstinacy, but out of fear that if he moved too suddenly, my gun might have gone off in his mouth.

So we lay there, me on top of him as his brother approached, the light from his torch bouncing off the trees around us. He came to a halt only a few feet from where we lay. I tried not to breathe, not to make a sound. I pushed the barrel of the gun further into Marc's mouth. He stayed quiet. The thought of trying to fly away came into my mind - but I would have to remove my jacket, fold my shirt and take the gun out of Marc's mouth while doing all of that. I couldn't risk it.

"Marc! Marc! Where are you? Call to me, buddy!" Steve shouted into the silent night. The light from his torch bounced around again and for a moment, it lit up the ground only inches from my face. I readied myself for the moment that his light fell directly on us, but it never did. He stood there for a few moments longer, and then headed off at speed in the opposite direction.

I continued to lie on top of Marc, my gun rammed into his mouth until I felt that Steve was far enough away.

"C'mon, get up," I whispered into his ear. I pulled him to his feet and kept my gun tightly between his teeth, my other hand pulling him along by his shoulder. Our progress was slow, but I daren't risk putting on my torch. I guessed that Steve was some way behind us, but it was dark so I couldn't be sure.

I continued to shove Marc forward as quietly as possible but every few yards our position would be given away by the sound of snapping branches under our feet. Then all at once there was a *BANG*, a flash of light, and the sound of a bullet whizzing past my right ear.

"Jeezus!" I cried out, yanking my gun from Marc's mouth. I fired a shot blindly off in the direction I had been shot at. I then began to run, dragging my prisoner along beside me. I didn't know if it was because his hands were still cuffed behind his back or what, but he seemed to be dragging his feet and stumbling and falling at every opportunity.

"Get Up! *Get up!*" I hissed at him, pulling him up from the ground by his hair. He howled in pain and another bullet whizzed past me, burying itself in the trunk of a nearby tree.

"C'mon!" I roared and forced him forward.

I could hear the sounds of breaking branches close behind me now and the laboured sound of Steve's breathing as he panted in the darkness like a giant dog. I guessed he was only yards from my heels and no longer looked like a human. I could sense we were coming to the edge of the wooded area as the trees began to thin and become less dense. I was relieved that we were reaching the road, but with fewer trees, I had less cover.

I made one last push and shoved Marc on with all the energy I had left. We reached the clearing and I could see the road and my car about two hundred yards ahead of us. Another shot whipped past and tore into the ground a couple of feet in front of us with an explosion of earth. Without even glancing back, I pointed the gun behind me and fired. I knew instantly I had missed my target as the sound of paws rushing over the woodland floor was deafening in my ears.

I reached the car and fumbled with the key in the lock. Marc was now lying face up on the road, his hands cuffed behind him. Out of the woods and beneath the pale light of a crescent moon, I could see that he too looked more like a wolf than a man now as he tried to work himself free from the cuffs. He barked and howled. I took hold of his shoulder and dragged him round to the other side of the car. I glanced over the bonnet to see Steve come bounding out of the woods. He had ditched the gun, his hands now empty and shaped like two giant paws. He leapt into the air towards the car.

I yanked open the passenger door, and fought desperately to push Marc between the back and front seats of the car. He thrust his jaws at me as he tried to bite my face. The car shook violently and I looked up to see Steve crouching on the roof. He swiped at me with one razor-sharp paw, and then he was flying backwards through the air. I ducked to avoid his paw. When I looked over the bonnet of the car again, I saw a giant black winged creature spinning through the air, as it slashed, ripped, and bit at Steve. Marc continued to bark as I slammed the car door against his legs. He instinctively drew them into the car, and I shut the door, imprisoning him inside. I looked back to see Steve go racing away up the road. The winged creature I had seen hovered momentarily in the air as if deciding whether to go after him or not, then turned to face me.

"Rom?" I breathed. "What are you doing here?"

"Come to save your sorry arse," he said, dropping out of the sky and landing on the road. With his wings disappearing back inside him, he strode towards me.

"I was right about Marc and his brother," I said.

Rom looked me up and down. I stared down at myself and could see I was covered in blood, puke, twigs, leaves, and dirt. "What in the name of sweet Jesus..." he started, his mouth hanging wide open.

"Marc murdered my friend, Pen," I told him, taking the DVD from my jacket pocket. "It's all on this disc."

Chapter Twenty-Three

Murphy

We drove home, Marc lying face down in the back of the car, barking and howling all the way. At the police station, Marc was taken to the cells, while I sat in Rom's office, sipping at a hot mug of coffee. Rom sat away from me, silently watching the DVD I had found.

I ached all over and my head hurt. Not through any injury, cut, or bruise, and I had many, but because of the knowledge that Pen was dead was finally seeping its way into my consciousness. Back at her house I'd been too preoccupied fighting to save my own life and bringing the DVD and Marc to Rom. But now as I sat, bent forward, the realisation that my friend had gone, had been *murdered*, hammered away at my mind like a blunt axe. I wanted to be strong, I wanted to be able to accept I would never speak to or see her again, because the quicker I did, the sooner the agonising wound her death had created inside of me would be healed.

The urge to cry was too strong to resist. I felt as if my heart had been torn from my chest and repeatedly stamped on. Hot tears ran from my swollen eyes again and streamed down my cheeks. I bent forward and sobbed in pain. Those images of Pen thrashing about on the floor with Marc on top of her, hands round her throat, kept forcing their way into my mind like splinters of broken glass.

The mug of coffee I had been holding slipped from my fingers and onto the floor, as I rocked back and forth, clutching my head in my hands. I wanted those images of Pen suffering out of my mind. I couldn't bear to look at them anymore. But they just kept coming, slicing away at my brain, and it was agony.

I hadn't seen Rom get up and approach me, but I knew he was there, standing right next to me. He gently squeezed my shoulder with one of his huge hands.

"Go on, son, let it all out," he whispered. "There was nothing you could have done, nothing any of us could have done. By the looks of things, your friend died over a week ago."

"Her name was, Pen. And she wasn't just a friend to me..." I croaked.

"I don't want to know what kind of relationship you had with her..." Rom cut over me, as if trying to protect himself in some way.

"She was like a sister to me..." I sobbed.

"Sure she was," Rom soothed. "And you were a good brother. You risked your life to find out what had happened to her, even though she was a wolf."

I wiped my running nose and eyes on the back of my sleeve and sat back in the chair and looked at Rom.

"Pen's body is in the basement," I told him.

"What basement?" he asked, looking confused.

"You'll find Pen's body in the basement at the Ooze bar. I'm sure that's where Marc has hidden her."

"What makes you so sure?"

"Just a feeling – a hunch," I assured him. "I was right though, wasn't I...about Pen, I was right."

Rom looked away from me and I could sense his embarrassment and shame.

"Yeah you were, kiddo, you were." His gaze met mine again and he said, "I'm sorry, I should've helped you sooner."

"It won't bring Pen back, and like you said – however painful it may be, Pen was dead long before I got that note," I said.

"What note?" he asked suspiciously.

141

Realising what I had said, and not wanting to break my promise to Annie, I shook my head and said, "It was nothing, nothing at all."

Rom sniffed, looked at me, and changing the subject, he said, "So you gonna come check out this basement with me, or not?"

I shook my head. The thought of finding Pen's naked, dead body made me want to throw up again. I didn't want to see her battered and bruised body, the strangulation marks about her neck, her lips swollen and purple. I wanted to remember her beautiful as she stared up at those magical moving pictures in The Hollows.

There's no place like home! I could almost hear Dorothy whisper in my ear – but it was Pen's voice I could hear.

"I'm not coming with you. I'm gonna go home," I said to Rom and left his office.

The sun was peeking over the horizon when I eased open the front door to the small house I shared with Chloe. The night's events had caught up with me and I needed sleep. As I had crossed town, I had fought a constant battle with my eyelids as they continually tried to slide shut. I had almost swerved from the road twice, but I had pushed on, my most immediate need wasn't to fall into the warm embrace of Chloe, but to fall into bed.

As I stepped into the hall, I noticed that another white envelope had been tucked under the door. I picked it up and removed the folded piece of paper from inside. The handwriting was identical as that scribbled on the last two letters. I wondered what else Annie had to tell me. It read:

I think we should forget about each other...until I'm ready to contact you again.

I was too tired to read and re-read her note and pontificate on its meaning. So I placed it back into its envelope and tucked it into my jacket pocket. I closed the door and went upstairs. Chloe was asleep on her side, making those gentle breathing sounds she always made when deep in sleep. I kissed her on the cheek and lay down next to her. I was asleep before I'd even removed my clothes.

Rom obviously didn't like the idea of me sleeping, as it was the second time in the last two days he had disturbed my sleep by calling me on the telephone. I woke suddenly, and for a moment I couldn't remember where I was. The room was in total darkness, so I fumbled around for the bedside lamp. I switched it on and stared at my watch through bleary eyes. I blinked twice when I saw the time. It was 22:37 hours – I had slept through the entire day and evening. Chloe must have decided to leave me be and rest, and I guessed she was working a nightshift.

The phone continued to ring beside me, so I picked up the receiver and said, "Hello?"

"Murphy, is that you?" he said.

"Yes, it's me," I replied.

"I've been trying to get hold of you all day!" he barked.

"Sorry, but I've been sleeping," I explained.

"Look, I just wanted you to know that we drew a blank at the bar...you know, in the basement. Your friend's body wasn't there."

So it was true – Pen really had been murdered. I'd hoped it had been part of some hideous dream nightmare, I thought to myself as I tried to comprehend what Rom was telling me.

"That's strange, because Marc definitely hadn't wanted me going down in the basement the other day when I paid him a visit," I said.

"Yeah, and I know why!" he boasted. "The place was full of stolen property. Looks like Steve, Marc's younger brother, has been responsible for a spate of robberies that have been taking place over the last few months. So thanks to you and one of your hunches, the local cops have managed to solve over thirty robberies."

"I'm pleased for them," I said dryly.

"I sent a couple of the team to go track Steve down. They brought him in this afternoon," Rom explained.

"But what about Pen's body?" I pushed.

There was a pause on the other end of the line and I could hear Rom clearing his throat. "I haven't had much luck there, I'm afraid. Neither Marc or his brother is talking – they ain't saying anything. I got some of the team to take 'em both round the back of the station and give 'em both a slap – but they still didn't talk. So I went and paid 'em a little visit in their cells. Even when I had young Steven's nuts squeezed so tight in my hand I thought his eyes were gonna pop straight outter his head – he still wouldn't say anything!"

I mentally recalled the size of Rom's huge hands and even my eyes began to water at the thought of him crushing Steve's nuts with them.

"Look, it sounds like you've got a grip of things…" I never intended that to sound like some cheap punch-line, but Rom roared with laughter down the phone.

"That's the way, son, keep looking on the funny side of things. I'll have those bastards talking before long…I promise, when I've finished with 'em, they'll be wishing they'd been castrated at birth! And when they do start talking, you'll be the first to know," he assured me.

"Thank-you," I said and hung up the phone.

144

Chapter Twenty-Four

Murphy

Rom never did manage to incite Marc or Steve to confess where and how they had disposed of Pen's body, however much encouragement he gave them. They probably believed that if her body was never found they wouldn't be found guilty of her murder by the Elders. So both went to trial without saying a single word about the death of Pen. Then again, they didn't need to, as everything the Elders needed to find them guilty was on that DVD.

During the days after losing Pen, I told Chloe everything that had happened – well, almost everything and it was becoming harder and harder for me to keep my true identity from her. There was never going to be a trial in a courthouse, with a judge and jury, defence lawyers and prosecutors. The case would be held in secret, below ground – deep within The Hollows. It wasn't only that which made me feel like a fraud. Even though Pen had gone, I knew I was still in love with her – however much it had been forbidden. Chloe deserved someone better than me. She deserved a man who would love her – she needed to be with a human. I would only bring her heartache and I couldn't do that to her. So one evening as she left for her nightshift as a paramedic, I sat at the kitchen table and started to write her a letter. However much I tried, I couldn't find the words I needed to say. Whatever I wrote would only be a lie. So taking the letter Pen had first written to me when she had made contact again – the letter which spoke of The Hollows, the Fountain of Souls, the Vampyrus, and the Lycanthrope – I placed it open on the table for Chloe to find. It explained everything. Then, taking the slippers she had bought for me that Christmas, as I wanted something to remember her by, I turned out the lights and left her. I wondered if we would ever meet again – something might *push* us back together.

Rom moved me to another station, but I kept in touch with him. We talked about possible locations of where Marc and Steve may have disposed of Pen's body. The fact that they remained silent seemed to me to be the cruellest part of their crime. I found it impossible to even begin to deal with my grief without being able to bury my friend and say a final goodbye to her. I think they both understood this, and refused to give up their secret to inflict on me as much pain as possible.

Rom surprised me by suggesting I get together with some of Pen's friends and hold a small wake for her. I didn't really know too many of Pen's friends, only the ones she had briefly introduced to me on my visits to see her. The only friend of Pen's I really knew was Annie, but in her last note to me, she had asked that I forgot all about her. I planned on respecting her wish.

Two weeks after discovering the DVD, Marc and his brother Steve were taken before the Elders. The short hearing was held in one of the many temples deep in The Hollows. The room looked something like a small chapel, with walls that had been carved out of red rock. Clusters of candles burnt in each corner, casting long, eerie shadows over the walls that flickered as if they were alive. The Elders, stood in their hooded grey robes, faces covered. They cleared Steve of the murder of Pen but found him guilty of the attempted murder of me, a Vampyrus police officer, while trying to capture a rogue Lycanthrope. He was given life imprisonment in The Hollows. Marc was found guilty of murdering Pen and was sentenced to death by decapitation – one of the only sure ways of killing a Lycanthrope. As the Elders stated his fate, their childlike voices echoed chillingly off the stone walls of the temple.

On hearing the sentences passed down, I looked across the makeshift courtroom at Marc and Steve, who stood next to one another looking gaunt and pale, their hands manacled to a chain that looped about their waists. As Marc heard his fate, he howled at the hooded Elders and rattled his chains.

Rom began to chuckle. The Elders turned their covered faces towards him, and Rom's laughter faded. I thought I would feel some sense of satisfaction, some form of closure on hearing their sentences, but in truth, I didn't feel anything. I was numb at the thought of all the lives that had been ruined, theirs included. Marc's death wouldn't bring Pen back.

Marc and Steve were escorted from the courtroom and back to their cells. I was about to leave, when one of the Elders spoke from beneath their hood.

"Constable Murphy," the Elder said in its childish voice. "We heard what the female Lycanthrope claimed on that disc before she was murdered."

I turned back to face them.

"She said she *loved* you," another of them spoke. "And said she always had."

"I can explain..." I started.

"You had better not have *mixed* with the wolf, Constable," the Elder said. Although its voice sounded like that of a nine-year-old girl, it had a menacing and threatening tone to it. "You were obviously close to this female wolf. If it wasn't for the fact she is dead now, you too would be facing trial here today."

"But..." I started again.

"We're not interested in your excuses, Constable," said another, a harsh screeching tone to its voice. "Keep your distance from the wolves – don't be tempted by them."

"I won't be," I whispered back.

"We'll be watching your career with interest," the one with the girl-like voice warned.

Outside the courthouse, Rom approached me and patted me on my back. "Well, kiddo, looks like justice has been done. It's a shame that both of 'em won't be getting the chop, but one outter two ain't bad."

"I'm just glad that it's all over," I said.

"You'll come on the big day, won't you?" Rom said.

"What big day?"

"You know, the day they hold numb-nuts down and chop off his head!" and he made a swiping motion through the air with the flat of his hand.

On realizing what he was talking about, I shook my head and said, "No, I don't think I'll bother…"

"Hey, you got to! I'll make sure we get front row seats…" Rom started enthusiastically.

"I'll see you around," I said, slowly walking away.

Chapter Twenty-Five

Murphy

The day before Marc's execution, I got up early and made breakfast, which I sat and ate alone in the tiny flat I had rented above ground. Since Pen's death, I had thrown myself back into my career and decided to study for my sergeant's exam. I thought it might be a welcome distraction from everything that had happened. I showered, and looking in the cracked mirror above the sink, I could see my hair had grown greyer in colour, and I now had streaks of silver through it. I was only twenty-three. I stood, wrapped in my bathrobe, and trembled in the cold. Christmas was only a few weeks away again, and the first flurries of snow had started to fall. I headed to the kitchen to make a hot coffee. It was then I saw the envelope sticking out of the letterbox like a white tongue, and I pulled it free. My name had been scribbled across the front of it. I ripped it open and pulled out the folded piece of paper that had been tucked inside. It read:

I think it's safe for us to meet again. Pen once told me about the lake. Come tonight.

I hadn't thought of Annie in a while and was shocked to have suddenly heard from her again. *Why does she want to meet up again?* I wondered to myself. Maybe she wanted to meet one last time before Marc was executed? After all, with Marc only hours from his own death, and with Steve serving a life sentence, Annie probably felt it safe enough to meet up with me again.

Receiving the letter had set me off-course somehow, and instead of hitting the study books, I anxiously spent the next hour or two pacing back and forth around the house, my mind once more full of memories of Pen. I felt as if that letter had bewitched me, filling my head again of my friend's murder. Part of me was brimming with excited curiosity at meeting Annie again and finding out what it was that she wanted, but the other part of me resented her for coming back into my life and cutting open the stitching that I had used to seal up those wounds. But maybe that was the problem – perhaps I had never really tended to those wounds and had just fixed them up with Band-Aids. I wondered if Annie hadn't done the same. Maybe by meeting with her tonight, hours from our nemesis's demise, we would both find permanent healing.

I left for the forest, which surrounded the lake, in late afternoon. I parked my car some way off, as there was nothing other than a dirt track. I made my way down to the lake on foot, and as I pulled the collar of my jacket up against the cold, it started to snow. I made my way over the familiar ground and it dawned on me that I hadn't been back to the lake since Pen was sent away all those years ago. The forest and the lake with its thick, red waters had always been there but I had kept away. As I neared the lake again, I felt a certain amount of anxiety, and an overpowering sense of regret. Maybe I should have come back from time to time, sat on my own and enjoyed the memories of Pen and me. Perhaps I should have visited on her birthday and laid some flowers on the lake, perhaps...perhaps...perhaps. I hadn't done any of these things, and in my heart, I knew why I had avoided this place. I had found it too painful to return without my friend. This had been our place, our secret hideaway, where we had both fallen in love. It had been our playground, our utopia, our sanctuary – and without Pen, I believed it would feel lifeless, dead, just like her. We had enjoyed this place together, not alone.

I pulled out the torch I had brought with me and peered curiously around. To my surprise, it hadn't really changed at all. I passed the light over the area where we had once sat on the shore and skimmed pebbles across the red water. I stood and watched as thick flakes of snow seesawed lazily to and fro in the glow of my torch. I recalled how it had often snowed during the many hours that Pen and I had spent together down here. I remembered the last time that we had been here together. That had been the night she had fled at the sound of her father seeking her out. I could see us sharing that kiss. I could hear myself telling Pen I loved her.

As I stood and recalled all of those wonderful, yet painful memories, my eyes began to sting and then fill with tears. My shoulders shook uncontrollably as I began to sob, releasing months of pent-up anguish.

"I miss you, Pen," I whispered.

It was then I heard the sound of movement from the trees behind me. I wiped my eyes and peered into the darkness.

"Annie?" I called into the night. "Annie is that you?"

I then saw movement. A figure stepped out from between the snow-laden spruces and pines. I went to shine my torch in that direction but it slipped from between my fingers and dropped to the ground.

The figure came closer and I fumbled around for the torch. The tips of my fingers brushed over it. I snatched it up and shone it directly into the face of the approaching figure. On seeing their face, my legs gave out from beneath me and I fell backwards into the snow.

"Hello again, Jim," she said, holding out her hand towards me.

Shaking uncontrollably, and wondering if I was dreaming, I reached out and took hold of Pen's hand.

Chapter Twenty-Six

Murphy

Pen looked at me, her eyes bright and keen. Her long, blond-white hair trailed about her shoulders in thick waves. She wore a thick, white fur coat which trailed about her feet. The collar was up, nestling against the sides of her face.

"Pen?" I breathed, unable to believe it was really her. "Pen, is it *really* you?"

As if to prove to me that it was truly her and that she was very real, Pen threw her arms around me. "It's me, Jim, it's really *me*," she whispered in my ear. Her breath felt warm against the side of my face. I pulled away from her.

"But how? You're meant to be dead."

Then without saying another word, she took me by the hand and led me into the forest. Silently, we made our way through the trees until we came to a thick brush of undergrowth. Some snow had managed to work its way through the leafy canopy above us, and had covered the bushes. Gently, Pen pushed them aside, revealing a small circular area which offered shelter from the cold and the snow. Pen faced me and looked deep into my eyes. There was so much I wanted to say. So much I wanted to ask. Before I'd the chance to say anything, Pen leant forward and kissed me on the mouth. Her lips were soft. I closed my eyes and kissed her back. Gently at first, then more deeply. Her tongue felt like velvet inside my mouth. Pen pulled me close as I lost my hands in her hair. Her coat fell open and I could feel her naked body against me, which only heightened my desire for her. As we kissed, Pen pulled my jacket and shirt free. Then, fumbling with a growing passion, Pen unfastened my belt, pulling my jeans and shorts down over my hips. I kicked off my boots, then stepped out of my clothes. I placed my hands inside her coat, and cupped one of her soft breasts in my hand. Pen let her coat slip from her shoulders where it fell to the leaf-covered ground. As we continued to cover each other in kisses, we lowered ourselves onto the leafy ground, using her coat like a blanket. Pen rolled me onto my back and climbed on top of me. Slowly, we began to make love and it felt like I had waited a lifetime for this moment. I placed my hands around her back, pulling her down onto me. She worked her hips gently in a rocking motion, and I kissed her neck, face, breasts, anywhere I could.

"I love you," she murmured in my ear.

"I love you more, Pen," I breathed, moving my hips in time with hers. And even though I knew what we were doing was wrong – forbidden – it only increased my desire. I pushed the sound of the Elders' warning from my mind and gave myself completely to Pen. How could something which felt so beautiful be a crime? Then, as I ran my fingertips down the length of her spine as she continued to move faster and faster on top of me, I no longer felt smooth, cold skin, but soft, warm fur. I opened my eyes a fraction and could see that Pen's body was covered in a fine coat of pure white fur. She threw her head back and the softest of howls escaped from between her red lips. She looked more beautiful than any woman I had ever seen and she excited me. My heart raced in my chest and my head spun as my own claws shot from my fingertips, my fangs protruded from my gums, and my wings tried to free themselves from under me. She looked down into my face, both us now as we were meant to be – in our true form – Vampyrus and Lycanthrope.

"You truly are beautiful," I whispered.

"How beautiful?" she murmured.

"I'll show you," I said, easing her off me.

Gently, I lowered myself over her, as she wrapped her legs around my back, and I wrapped my arms round her. Locked together as if we were just one being, I made love to her. My wings sprung from my back, and they draped over us, hiding us from the rest of the world. The world which forbid our love for each other, made it feel dirty and wrong – unnatural. We cried out as one, then collapsed in each other's arms. With her coat beneath us, and my wings wrapped over us, we held each other tight. How I had longed for this moment. For the first time in my life, I felt a kind of peace wash over me.

With her head nestled against my chest, and my face lost in her hair, I said, "I don't understand what's going on here. I saw you die with my own eyes, Pen."

"I thought I was dead, too, until I woke up suddenly to find myself wrapped up tightly in a blanket, in the dark and on my own," she whispered.

"So Marc didn't murder you?" I asked. "This is not some dream that I'm going to wake up from?"

"It's not a dream," she said, easing herself around in my arms so she could look into my face. "Marc thought he had murdered me, and still does, but I got away."

"But how...? Where have you been...? Who else knows you're still alive?" My head started to hurt as I tried to play catch-up.

"Okay, I'll tell you everything...you might not like what you hear...but I had to do it, Jim...I had to do it," she said, staring at me.

"Do what?" I asked.

"Pretend I've been dead all this time."

"What are you saying? That the whole thing has been some elaborate con?" I shook my head disbelievingly.

Pen broke my gaze and said, "Yes...but, Jim, I had to do

it."

"So where's Annie? What part did Annie have to play in all of this?" The realization of what was happening and what had gone on was slowly seeping in and I was becoming angry – *hurt*.

"Annie – she didn't play any part in this...like everyone else, she thinks I'm dead," Pen explained.

"But the notes? She wrote letters to me...helping me..." I could see Pen slowly shaking her head at me.

"No, Jim, Annie never sent those letters...I did...they were all from me."

"All of them?" I asked in utter shock.

"All of them," she nodded, lowering her eyes as if in shame.

Feeling as if I had been tricked, deceived by her, I eased my way from her, stood up, and began to put my clothes on and went back out into the forest.

"I thought you'd be pleased to see me," Pen said, taking her coat and placing it about her shoulders and following me.

"Pleased to see you?" I laughed with tears standing in my eyes. "Do you know what I've been through for you? *Do you have any idea?"* I shouted.

Pen looked at me and shook her head.

"I was attacked...fucking shot at...God knows how many times! My Inspector thought I was fucking deranged...I had to sit and watch my best friend in a snuff-movie...put up with months of fucking anguish at the thought of you dying...only to find out I have been lied to...been deceived...but do you know what hurts most of all, Pen?" I barked at her.

She looked at me and shook her head numbly again.

"To be lied to by you...to be *deceived* by you. How could you be so *fucking cruel?"* I spat.

It felt as if my whole being, my whole existence had

been turned upside down. I wanted to feel relief, pleasure, sheer joy that she was still alive, but instead, I felt only anger and hatred for her.

"I'm sorry, Jim…I really am…but I had to. Marc was hurting me, he was stealing off me…he was *destroying* me."

"Why didn't you come to me, I would've *helped you!*" I said.

"I couldn't. Marc said that if he so much as got a whiff that I had involved you, he would have killed me. And besides, I wanted you to be proud of me…I wanted you to think that I had made a success of my life."

"Pen, I would have been proud of you whatever…" I started.

"I looked at your life and all of your dreams had come true," Pen cut in. "You had met a beautiful girl; you became a cop and were leading a full and exciting life. The Lycanthrope aren't meant to achieve anything with their lives. We are just a bunch of murderous criminals, or so the Vampyrus believe. I wanted to be different. I wanted to prove to you that I was different. The Ooze Bar proved I was making a success of my life – that I didn't want to be a criminal like my father, uncle…"

I listened as Pen told me how Marc had strolled into The Ooze Bar one day looking for work. He had been charming, funny and delightful at first, and Pen had fallen in love with him. So Pen had taken him on, and at first she thought Marc had some good ideas of how they could improve the bar and he seemed like a really hard worker. Then Steve was brought in as chef, with the intention of making the bar more of a success.

"When I asked Marc what cooking experience his brother had," Pen explained, "he told me that he had worked in lots of kitchens preparing food. What I didn't know then, and didn't find out until it was too late, was Steve had worked in plenty of kitchens but they had all been while serving time in prison in The Hollows."

When I discovered this, I confronted Marc, and for my trouble, I got a punch in the face.

"And that's when the violence started and the truth came out. I learnt that my father had given me away to Marc's father in a card game years ago. To Marc that meant not only was my body his, but everything I owned, too. He didn't love me. I was just a possession. I'm a wolf just like them, and at first I fought back, but I didn't stand a chance against the two of them."

"You should have *come* to me, Pen," I told her again.

"Like I said, I couldn't."

"So what did you do?"

"One night I was lying in bed, most of the violence started in bed. Marc would come home from the café, angry and spiteful. Marc was incredibly jealous, his jealousy bordered on paranoia. He would accuse me of picking human men up and taking them back to the house for sex while he was working at the bar. He often accused me and you of being lovers. He had got it into his head we had been more than just friends when we were kids and he told me that I was never to see or speak to you again."

"What did you say?"

"I told him to go fuck himself," she half-smiled.

"What did he say to that?" I asked, although I already knew the answer.

"He attacked me. He threw me onto the bedroom floor and started to strangle me. All the time he was screaming at the top of his voice, '*You fucked him! You fucked him – didn't ya?*' And when I tried to tell him we were just friends, he rammed paper into my mouth and down my throat until I passed out."

The images of that video swam back into the front of my

mind and my initial anger that I had felt for Pen turned to Marc.

"When I woke up," Pen continued to explain, "Marc had gone, so I seized my chance and fled from the house and ran out into the night. I didn't know where to go, I didn't know who to turn to, and so I went to Annie's."

Pen told me how she had cried in Annie's arms as she told her everything. Annie had begged her friend to go to the police, but what she didn't know was that Pen was a werewolf. I learnt that Pen stayed with Annie for a couple of nights until she thought it was safe to go home again.

It was then that Pen started to receive letters from the bank and the brewery, who demanded money for unpaid debts. Pen also found credit cards in her name hidden under the counter at the bar. Pen told me how she had telephoned the credit card companies and they assured her the cards did belong to her. Marc and his brother had been getting cards in her name and Pen was horrified and scared when she discovered they had run up debts of £15,000, £19,000, and £21,000 on different credit cards.

Pen explained her initial confusion as she considered why they needed so much money and what it had been spent on. It was only by chance one day, Pen had gone down into the basement to change a keg where she found Marc and Steve using heroin. Marc and Steve said that it helped them fight their curse.

"It was then I realised I had been unknowingly supporting their drug addiction," Pen said. "I felt trapped and overwhelmed by them. I didn't know how to get them out of my life. I knew that if I didn't, they would drag me down with them, or worse, Marc would end up killing me."

We walked back to the lake. The snow had begun to ease a little. I looked at Pen as she started to talk again.

"I knew I had to do something and it was you who gave

me the idea."

"How?" I asked.

"It came to me one day when we were talking on the phone. You were telling me all about your adventures at work and how you spy on wolves...you know...what's the word? Surveillance? You told me all about those dinky little cameras you used. I got myself one, and as you now know, I hid it in my ruby slippers in that display cabinet," Pen said.

"Wasn't that a bit risky? Marc could have found it," I said.

"You were hiding them from experienced criminals and they never spotted them. Marc was a violent, small-time thug who was always drunk and stoned. He would've never spotted it. I put it there for insurance, really. I'd turn it on every night before I went to bed. I was scared that one night he might go too far and kill me. At least then, there would be some evidence of it. It wouldn't matter that I was a wolf once I was dead, but it would have mattered to Marc if you and your cop friends had found the recording. Anyway, that night...the night I *died*...he came home in another drunken rage and attacked me again."

"I saw what happened on the DVD," I said. "But you looked dead. It looked as if he had *killed* you."

Pen pulled her coat tight about her naked frame. "The next thing I knew was when I woke up, in the dark, wrapped in a blanket with my throat feeling raw," she said. "I knew I was in a vehicle and could tell it was travelling at speed. I guessed I was in the back of Steve's truck as it was cold and I was outside. I didn't know how long I had been unconscious for, but I guessed it had been for a while from snippets of conversation I could hear every now and then between Marc and his brother. 'Why are we bringing her all the way up here? We've been going for hours,' I heard Steve ask Marc."

"Where were they taking you?" I asked Pen.

"I wasn't sure, but I was scared of what they were planning to do with me," she said.

"Didn't you try and escape?"

"The vehicle stopped a couple of times, I guess at traffic signals, and I did consider uncoiling myself and jumping out the back of the vehicle, but they would have seen me and then finished me off properly," Pen explained.

"So what did you do?"

"I waited. I didn't know what else I could've done. Eventually, we stopped and I heard them climb out of the cab and come to the back of the vehicle. I could hear them talking clearly now. 'How do you know this is the right place?' Steve asked Marc. 'Because no one ever comes out here other than wolves,' Marc told him. I couldn't believe what I had heard. I knew they had brought me here," Pen said, looking over her shoulder at the forest.

"Here?" I asked, startled. "But why all the way out here?"

"Like Marc said, these forests and the lake is secret from the rest of the world. There was very little chance my body would be found here by anyone other than another wolf," Pen explained. "They lifted me out of the back of the truck and between them, they carried me through the forest and dumped me back in those bushes."

"What happened next?" I asked.

"It was freezing cold, but I stayed wrapped in that old blanket for as long as I could," Pen said. "I lay there until I heard the engine of Steve's truck start up then drive away."

"What did you do then?" I asked incredulously.

"I went home," Pen said. "Back beyond the Fountain of Souls."

"But you said you would never go back there..."

"I know what I said, but I was desperate. I was in pain,

160

soaking wet and freezing cold. The night was fading and I knew that I had to get into hiding before it got light. Besides, my father had long since left the caves. I hadn't been back since I was girl. No one knew me."

"Why didn't you come to me? I would have helped you. We could have got everything sorted out once and for all. You had the DVD of Marc attacking you, we could have taken it to my Inspector, just like you had planned, and that would have been the end of it," I said.

Pen looked at me with her bright orange eyes and said, "I wanted Marc to *pay*, Jim. I wanted him to *suffer* for what he had done to me. Together, Marc and his brother had ruined The Ooze Bar and they had ruined *me*. I knew that while they thought I was dead, I was safe. So like Dorothy, I went home."

Chapter Twenty-Seven

Murphy

The night sky gave way and unleashed a blizzard of snowfall that almost engulfed us. Pen went back over to the bush and hurriedly yanked back the bramble and we forced our way back in. We hunkered down onto the ground where we had earlier made love. Pen sat opposite me, her knees drawn up beneath her coat.

She looked at me, then said, "It was while I was hiding out in the caves for those few days, I hatched my plan."

"And you decided to drag my sorry arse into this?" I whispered.

"I knew that if I could get you to realise I had suddenly gone missing, then you would start to nose around and ask questions," she said.

"So how did you get the notes to me? And who did you get to write them, as it wasn't your handwriting?" I asked her.

"In the dead of night, I would leave the caves. I would run through the forest, some blank sheets of paper, envelopes, and a pen in my pocket. I skulked about the back streets, keeping to the shadows and searching behind the stores, until I came across this old homeless guy hidden beneath a pile of cardboard boxes. He thought God had sent me from heaven when I offered him money to write me out four short notes. His spelling wasn't up to much, so I had to write down what I wanted in each one and then he copied them word for word. I realised that by the morning, after he had finished off the liquor he would have bought with the money I had given him, he probably wouldn't have even remembered me."

I couldn't believe Pen's cunning but secretly admired

her tenacity.

"While I still had the cover of darkness," she continued, "I headed over to your place and posted the first letter. And that was that, the ball was rolling and the rest was pretty much out of my hands."

Pen sat and stared at me, waiting for me to speak, to say anything.

"So the note posted under my hotel room door, that was you, too?" I eventually asked.

"Yes," she replied.

"How did you know I was staying there?"

Pen cupped her hands around her mouth and blew warm air over them.

"It was simple, Jim," she sighed. "There are only two hotels in town. One is a flea pit and the other half decent. I called the decent one, said I had a meeting with you but couldn't remember your room number. Simple. Then all I had to do was deliver the note."

"And the rest I know," I said thoughtfully. Then looking at her, I added, "So what happens now?"

"What do mean?" she asked right back.

"How are we gonna get outter this mess?"

"I'm not," she said flatly, staring me straight in the face.

"Pen, you can't go around for the rest of your life pretending you're dead," I snapped.

"Why not?"

"Because tomorrow night someone is gonna get their fucking head chopped off for a crime they haven't committed," I reminded her.

Pen looked away. "So what."

"*So what?*" I gasped. "You can't let Marc be executed for a crime he hasn't committed!"

"Yes, I can," Pen insisted. "He tried to kill me, and as far as he's concerned, he did."

"Are you fucking insane?" I exploded. "There's a world of difference between trying to murder you and *actually* murdering you!"

"Like what?" she asked stubbornly.

"Like you're still fucking alive, that's what!" I yelled at her.

"He deserves to die for what he did to me!" Pen hollered back.

"Look, Pen," I said, trying to remain calm. "You're gonna have to think of something...some way of coming back from the dead."

"Like what?" Pen sneered.

"I dunno...pretend that you've been suffering from amnesia for the last few months and you've only just remembered who you are," I suggested. I knew it was a crap idea, but my mind was scrambling to think of a good one.

"I don't believe you! Are you for real?" she mocked. "Do you really think anyone will buy that?"

"Well you'd better think of something, Pen, because I don't know if I can sit back and watch someone die – wolf or not – for something they haven't done," I warned.

"What are you saying? You gonna give me up?" she asked in disbelief.

"Have you got any idea what happens to someone when they go to the chopping block?" I whispered.

"They get decapitated!" she barked. "Tell me something I don't know."

"Don't be such a fucking wise-arse!" I snapped. "Before they take them down to the block, the guards stuff tampons up their arse and make them wear a fucking nappy because most of them crap themselves in fear! Why do you think the condemned have to wear one of those black face masks?" I

demanded.

"I don't know?" she shrugged as if unbothered by what I was telling her.

"Because when the axe passes through their necks, their eyes *explode* right out of their fucking skull!" I told her.

Pen looked away again and said, "You expect me to have pity for that arsehole! He tried to kill me! It was only by some freak miracle I survived."

"But that's the whole point, Pen, you did *survive!*" I took a deep breath, then in a calmer tone of voice, I tried to reason with her one last time.

"Look, Pen, if you let him go to the block, you ain't any better than him," I said. "You become a killer – the curse will get hold of you."

Pen remained quiet, and I hoped my reasoning had worked. Then after a moment or two, Pen screwed her hands into fists and shouted at me, "Fuck him! I'm not saying anything to help that son-of-a-bitch." Pen got up and went back out into the snow. I took a deep breath and went after her.

The snow was racing down at a pace and it was so thick and heavy, it took me a moment to locate Pen's whereabouts as she wore the white fur coat. I hurried over to her, snow pelting my face.

"Well, you've fixed this whole thing up real good, haven't you!" I bellowed.

Pen turned to face me, and with a wry smile playing at the corners of her lips, and her arms outstretched at either side of her, she stared straight into my eyes.

"I told you I was The Wizard of Ooze!" she laughed into the night.

"What do you mean?" I breathed, wondering if she hadn't gone insane.

"I was the man behind the curtain, pulling all the levers,

pressing all the buttons, just like the Wizard of Oz," Pen said.

"This isn't some sorta fairy tale, Pen, this is *real* life!" I barked at her. "You can't go through with this! I can't go through with it...I can't stand by and let it happen."

"If you're worried about your job, I'll never tell anyone that you knew!" she tried to bargain with me.

"It has nothing do with me being a cop!" I said, although in my heart I knew different.

I was a Vampyrus cop and that meant something to me. Just like my brother Peter had chosen to help others in his life, I wanted to do the same. I wanted to help the wolves stop killing – I didn't want to be responsible for the death of one of them, not if they hadn't committed the crime they had been accused of. That was breaking the rules and I didn't want to be a part of that. I wanted to be better than that.

So looking straight into Pen's eyes, I added, "I'll know that Marc didn't really murder you and I don't think I can live with that on my conscience! Pen, please...I don't want to have to give you up!"

Pen moved closer to me and touched my face with her hand. "Don't betray me, Jim."

"I love you, Pen. I always have, and for the last few months...every day I've wished you were still alive...but now I just wish you were dead."

Pen held me against her. "Jim, you can't mean that."

"What, you think we can just pick up from where we left off? The Elders, my Inspector, they all think you're dead and you may as well be. We can never see each other again if you go ahead with what you are planning to do," I said.

"I'm sorry for ever coming back. I never meant to hurt you." She wiped tears from her eyes.

Pen went to touch my hand but I pulled it away.

"I'm so sorry," she said, turning to leave.

"I'm sorry, too," I called after her.

Pen turned to look back at me. "What for?" she asked.

"For what I have to do," I said.

"Do whatever your heart tells you to do, Jim. But I'm not ever coming back. I'll check the classifieds in the Times newspaper on the first Monday of every month...if you ever need me...if you ever want anything...leave me a message under the name Lilly Blu," she said.

"I don't need you for anything, Pen...after all, you're dead," I shouted. At once I regretted what I had said, but once those words had escaped my lips, I couldn't pull them back. They just tossed, floated and got lost amongst the falling snow.

We looked at each other one last time and then she turned away, disappearing into the snowfall, the only sign she had ever been there, was her footprints in the snow. I turned and made my own as I headed slowly away in the opposite direction.

Chapter Twenty-Eight

Murphy

I walked all night. I couldn't go home. I was in shock. I knew what I had to do but didn't know if I could do it. Could I give up Pen? If I didn't, could I live with myself, knowing that I let an innocent man die?

I felt like screaming until my soul exploded. What had I ever done to deserve to be put in such a situation? I would have given my own life to be free of this burden.

I thought of Pen and all the misery Marc had put her through, and although I hated him for that, I still couldn't find in any part of my being a voice that said he should pay for that with his life.

I had been in law enforcement long enough to know what happened before and during the beheading. I knew by now, Marc would have been moved from his cell. He would be on constant suicide watch, his only visitors Vampyrus prison guards, and a Black Coat – perhaps my brother – who would ask to pray with him. I looked at my watch and realised that in a matter of hours, Marc would be given the opportunity to choose his last meal. What would he chose? I wondered.

An hour before his execution, Marc would be woken. His legs and arms would then be manacled and he would be walked slowly to the block.

As these thoughts twisted inside my head, I lurched forward and vomited violently into the curb. Sick swung from my mouth in long, ropey streams and I wiped it away with my sleeve. I continued to walk for hours in the falling snow. Around and around in circles, with no direction, lost inside myself. I desperately felt the urge to share my burden, to share it with someone else, to give it to them – dump it on them and let them make the decision for me – then I could blame them – whatever the outcome – it would be their fault, not mine.

But in my heart, I knew it was my burden, and however heavy and painful, I had to carry it on my own. What was I to do? If I told Rom or the Elders about what Pen had done, she would be hunted down by them. She would face jail deep in The Hollows and I knew that would kill her. But if I said nothing and the truth were ever discovered – I too would be imprisoned or worse. I had already been warned by the Elders and Rom about any feelings I might have for Pen. If they discovered we shared such a dark secret, then I too would be executed. So my dilemma, save Marc and condemn Pen, or say nothing, sending Marc to the block and as a result of my silence, destroy myself.

I looked at my watch and knew I had only a few hours to save Marc or destroy Pen. The urge to share the agony of my nightmare was overwhelming, but who could I share my burden with, without destroying them also? Who could I trust to never say a word, whatever my decision? Who could I tell who would sit and listen and not judge me?

I then heard Pen, whispering inside my head, *There's no place like home! There's no place like home!*

So that's what I did, I went home, to the place where I was first given life, to the arms that first cradled me as I took my first breaths of life. I went home to my mum.

Her room, in the temple where she was being cared for, was small and smelt of peppermint and urine. I walked silently over to where she was seated, motionless and grey, staring blankly at the wall.

I kissed her cheek gently and said, "Hello, Mother."

She didn't respond, not even her eyelids flickered. It was as if I wasn't there. I hunkered down at her feet, took hold of her hand, pressed it against my cheek, and began to sob. It was the first time I could recall ever truly needing my mum. The need for her love and understanding now was so great and overwhelming, I thought it would crush me.

As I sat there, her hand held in mine, I told her everything. I told her the story of my life, which she had missed so much of. I told her about my love for Pen, of everything we had been through together and the terrifying decision I was now faced with. All the while, she did not so much as flinch. Even as I cried and struggled to find the right words, she sat and stared blankly at the wall, her eyes wide open and her mouth ajar.

I looked at my watch and knew by now Marc would be eating his last meal.

"What should I do, mum?" I implored her. "Mum, help me!"

She remained silent, a small silver stream of drool sneaking from the corner of her mouth.

I pressed myself against her brittle legs and I ran her hand through my hair, pretending that she was gently soothing my pain away.

"Please tell me you'll love me, mum, whatever decision I make," I whispered.

Again she remained silent, locked in her own pain and loss.

I glanced at my watch again and knew Marc would now be dressed in a diaper and having his legs and wrists chained.

"Help me, mum," I sobbed, a deep well of anger now growing inside me for Pen. How could she have put me in this position? But hadn't I put myself in it? I had been warned about the Lycanthrope. I had been told that they were never to be trusted. I had promised I would never mix with a wolf.

In my mind's eye, I could see the observation tower filling up with those Vampyrus who liked to watch a good beheading of a wolf. I knew Rom would be there, jostling and shoving himself forward, so as to guarantee himself a front row seat.

"Please, mum, what should I do?'" I beseeched her.

Silence.

I could see Marc being slowly and methodically strapped in place over the block. Then once fully secured, being asked by the Vampyrus official if he would like to make a statement.

"Mum, I can't breathe!" I cried.

Silence.

By now they would be placing the black hood over Marc's head. The Vampyrus official would look once over at the Elders to see if a last-minute stay of execution would be issued.

"Mum..." I whispered, closing my eyes, knowing that by now the axe would be slicing through Marc's neck.

Silence.

I continued to sit at my mum's feet in a trance-like state, until I was dragged from it by a sound. It was faint but indisputable. I turned towards the noise to discover it was the sound of my mother gently sobbing.

"Mum, what have I done...?" I asked her.

Chapter Twenty-Nine

Kiera

Murphy sat across the room from me, his dead brother – my father – at his feet. I looked up and out of the window. The snow had stopped at last, and the sky had started to lighten in the distance. Dawn was only about an hour away. Murphy had been talking most of the night, as Potter and I sat and listened in silence. Potter sat on the opposite side of the room from me. In the light of the lamp, I could see that, although he still looked battered and bruised, the dark purple and black bruises which covered his face had paled to a dark green and sickly yellow. He sat forward in his seat and lit a cigarette. He blew smoke from his nostrils like a dragon. I looked away and back at Murphy. I was still angry at Potter. He had hurt me and still had a lot of explaining to do – but I wasn't yet ready to listen.

"Did you ever see her again?" I asked Murphy.

"Huh?" he said, looking up at me.

"Pen, did you see her again?"

"No," Murphy said with a gentle shake of his head. "But I did hear one last time from her."

"When?" Potter asked, flicking ash on the floor.

"About seven or eight weeks later," Murphy said, running his thick fingers through his unruly white hair. "I woke one morning to the sound of crying. It was soft, kinda muffled. I climbed out of bed in search of where it was coming from. It was still dark outside, but I followed the sound of the crying to my backdoor. Outside was a cardboard box, and the noise of the crying was coming from inside. Quickly, I took the box into my kitchen where it was warm. I opened it up, and to my shock, I found two babies. Both were no older than just a few weeks. They were wrapped together in one thick blanket. Placed on top of the blanket was an envelope, and across the front was written my name. With a pair of trembling hands, I tore it open. Then, almost falling onto one of the kitchen chairs, I read what was written on the sheet of paper tucked inside. It read:

Dear Jim, Please find help for our twin daughters. They are both very weak and sick. I'm so sorry to do this to you. Please let me know that they are okay by leaving a message like we agreed.

Forever in my heart – Pen."

Murphy stopped talking and lent forward in his seat. He looked older and tired.

"Meren and Nessa?" Potter said. "Your daughters are..."

"Like me," I whispered, looking opened-mouthed at Murphy.

"Yes," he nodded without looking up at me. "I took the two little baby girls from the box and held them in my arms, knowing they had been conceived in the forest the night Pen had come back. I knew that Vampyrus and Lycanthrope gestate for only six to eight weeks, and looking at the two babies in my arms, I knew that the timeframe was correct. Pen had been right, both our daughters were very sick. Their cries were weak, no more than gentle mewing. Their skin was so pale it was almost translucent. At first I didn't know what to do. Who did I turn to for help without giving up my secret that I had mixed with a wolf, and that the two babies were a result of that union? It was forbidden, remember. I couldn't bring them up. I didn't know how to make them well, and even if I did, how did I explain away the fact I was suddenly the father of two daughters? The Elders had said they would be watching me. Then, as I paced my kitchen floor, cradling the two sick babies to my chest, I remembered I had heard of two Vampyrus doctors who were trying to find a cure for those sick half-breeds who were born out of human and Vampyrus mixing.

"So, placing the babies back into the box, I raced across the country to the place known as Hallowed Manor where the two doctors named Ravenwood and Hunt carried out their work. As I handed them over to Doctor Hunt, he asked where the two children had come from. I told him I couldn't answer that. Ravenwood was more insistent, claiming that they wouldn't be able to help them if they didn't know the children's heritage. Not wanting to put my daughters' lives at risk, I told Ravenwood I believed the babies were a result of a human and Lycanthrope mixing. Both Hunt and Ravenwood looked at me, then quickly closing the box, Ravenwood raced into the back of the manor with them. Then gripping me by the shoulder, Hunt looked into my face and whispered, 'You must never tell anyone about this. Forget what happened here today. Forget about these two children.'

"I told Hunt that I would never be able to forget them, as they were my daughters. Hunt squeezed my shoulder as if in some way he understood. He then turned to head back into the manor to join Ravenwood. As he reached the huge front door, he turned and said, 'What are their names?'

"I didn't know? Had Pen named them? So looking back at Hunt, I said 'Meren and Nessa.' Hunt nodded and disappeared back into the manor and closed the door."

"But Meren and Nessa knew that you were their father," Potter said.

"Yes," Murphy nodded. "Hunt and Ravenwood were very good to me. They let me visit my daughters as they grew older. They were always very sick, weak, and fragile. But on good days, I would often take Meren and Nessa into the grounds which surrounded Hallowed Manor. When the

174

weather was warm, I would take them out to the summerhouse and read books to them. They were never really well enough to play games, but we enjoyed the time we spent together. Ravenwood and Hunt were very kind and kept my secret for me. I came to suspect – although I could never be sure – that Meren and Nessa weren't the only two Vampyrus-Lycanthrope half-breeds being cared for in that secret hospital hidden in the roof of Hallowed Manor. But like Hunt and Ravenwood had never really pressed me about my secret, I respected theirs. Then, when Meren and Nessa reached the age of about fifteen years, their health deteriorated to such a point that they became bedridden and never left that secret hospital ward again. Ravenwood and Hunt had my daughters fixed up to machines and other contraptions, but they were just keeping them barely alive. The girls stopped growing, stopped aging. They had died years ago – way before Sparky and Luke got their hands on them. I just couldn't let them go."

"Why not?" I whispered.

Then raising his head to look at me, Murphy said, "Because they were all I had left of Pen."

"Did she ever visit them?" Potter asked, rubbing his ribs with his hands.

"No," Murphy said. "Meren and Nessa asked about their mother, and I spoke of Chloe."

"Why?" I breathed.

"Because she would have made a better mother," Murphy said. "Over the years I left messages for Lilly Blu in the Times Newspaper just like Pen had told me to, but I never heard anything back from her. I checked the newspaper so often, it bordered on obsession. But Lilly Blu never replied. So to let go of her in a small way, I told Meren and Nessa about Chloe saying that she had passed over a few weeks after their births. It was a lie – but we were all living a lie, I figured. Did one more hurt?"

"But lies do hurt," I said, glancing down at my father's body, then back at Murphy.

Murphy drew a deep breath. Then, taking his pipe from his coat pocket, he lit it. Behind a haze of blue smoke, he started to talk again. "My brother was unaware of the double life I was leading, so when he came to me a few years later and told me of the secret relationship he was having with the wolf, Kathy Seth, I panicked. I was desperate for my brother not to fall into the mess I had. I couldn't tell him about what had happened to me, and how the unhappiness of mixing with a wolf had almost destroyed me and my life. Peter was in thick with the Elders, he had devoted his life to their teachings – he was a Black Coat, after all. So just wanting to protect him from the pain and misery that I knew lay in wait for him if he continued his secret relationship with Kathy Seth, I refused to help him. I told him to have nothing more to do with the wolves – to get shot of Kathy Seth and her son, Jack from his life. But like I had been in love with Pen, Peter loved Kathy and had come to love Jack as his son. But Peter told me he couldn't just walk away from Kathy as she was carrying his child. To hear this filled me with rage. I knew the pain and the suffering he had not only inflicted on himself, but on that unborn child, too. But I couldn't tell him that. I couldn't tell my brother how I knew that the child would be born sick and spend a lifetime of suffering and pain, hidden from the world in a makeshift hospital at the top of some remote manor house. So I grew angry with him, when really I was angry at myself. I drove both Peter and Kathy in my car to the forest which surrounds the secret lake. If she was going to give birth, then it would be safer for both of them if the baby were born in the caves behind the Fountain of Souls. But as we raced through the forest, Kathy went into labour early."

Murphy stopped talking, and looked across the room at me.

"So it is all true?" I whispered, feeling numb. "Everything Jack told me is true."

"You were stillborn," Murphy said softly. "Or so I first thought. I didn't know what to do. Your mother was bleeding heavily and Peter was a complete mess. Just like me, they believed you were dead. So I took you to the lake, wrapped you in my shirt, and hoped that my brother's secret would sink to the bottom of those dark waters. But you floated back to the surface again and started to cry. I just couldn't leave you. I didn't know what to do. I knew that my brother believed you to be dead, and I believed it would be best for him if he continued to think that. I didn't have the time to take you to the manor – not then; I had to get back to my brother. So I raced quickly away, leaving you in the care of one of my constables. I only intended for you, Kiera, to stay with Jessica for a day or two, until I had the chance to smuggle you away to Hallowed Manor. But when I returned, you weren't sick like my daughters. You seemed to be thriving. What would have been the point of sending you to be cared for by Hunt and Ravenwood? Much to my surprise you were a healthy baby. It would have been unfair of me to have taken you to them, where you would have spent your life as little more than a prisoner. I could also see Jessica had taken to you – she loved you as if you had been her own. I could have taken you from her – but there was no need – you were not weak, fragile, or dying. So I went away, your survival a secret. It was only a short time later I discovered the wolf, Jack Seth, was living with my brother. So it was then I came up with the idea of staging his suicide. But to get my brother to agree to such a thing I would have to convince him there was a better life waiting for him away from Kathy Seth and her son, Jack. So I told him about you, Kiera. I told him that you were still alive. He wept with joy. But we didn't have much time and he had to decide. I gave him an ultimatum. If I told him where I had hidden you, then he was to have nothing more to do with the boy Jack or his family. My brother, your father, said that it was impossible for him to choose as he had come to love Jack as a son. But, Kiera, you were his daughter – his flesh and blood – and I reminded him of that and he made his choice. He chose to be with you, Kiera, his beloved daughter. So between us, we staged his death, letting the boy Jack and the rest of the world believe that he was dead. I helped smuggle my brother away deep into The Hollows. When enough time had passed, he took the name Frank Hudson and made himself a life above ground. I had visited with your adoptive mother one last time and told her that your father would like to now have contact with his daughter. Jessica was unsure about my brother at first, fearing that he had come to take you away. But both Jessica and Peter were both Vampyrus and they found a way. If I'm to be honest, I think Jessica married Peter so she could remain with you, and it was probably the same for my brother. I can't be sure, as I never spoke with or saw my brother again after that. The Elders were watching me, remember, and I didn't want to lead them to my brother or Jessica, but more importantly to you, Kiera.

"Together, you were a perfect family. I didn't see Jessica again until she arrived in the Ragged Cove years later on her undercover assignment to find the Vampyrus who were feeding off the locals. As you know she went missing, only to discover later she had been hooked on the red stuff by Luke. Then I heard that my brother – your father – had died of cancer. So when the vacancy came up for a new recruit at my station in the Ragged Cove, I spoke to your trainer, Sergeant Phillips, and said I thought you would be perfect. Little did I know at the time he had his own plans for you. But I wanted to keep you close. I wanted to make sure you were safe and well – you were my brother's daughter – and that made me your uncle, although you were unaware of that. I'd heard whispers that you had the ability to *see* things and that you were very bright – the best recruit at training school. I wondered how long – if ever – it would take for you to become of age, to make the change into what you really were. I had no idea if you would be more wolf or Vampyrus. But what I really wanted to know was why you were so healthy, fit, and bright, when Meren and Nessa were nothing more than empty shells, being kept alive by the machines at Hallowed Manor," Murphy said.

A heavy silence hung over the room, and half of me expected Potter to come out with some wise-arse comment, but he didn't say anything. He just sat quietly in the corner as he, like me, tried to comprehend everything Murphy had said.

When I couldn't bear the silence any longer, I looked up at Murphy and said, "Why do you think I survived? Why didn't your daughters and any others like me survive?"

"I don't know," Murphy said with a slow shake of his head.

"I think I know why," I whispered thoughtfully.

"Why?" Murphy asked, squinting through his pipe smoke at me.

"I think it has something to do with the water in that lake," I told him. "You said I was dead, right?"

"Yes, or so I thought," Murphy said.

"But that's the difference. Can't you *see* that?" I asked. "Jack said something about the waters being filled with the souls of all the people the wolves have murdered. You told me once yourself that's why the fountain runs upwards, because it's all the dead souls going back to heaven."

"This is just getting weirder and weirder," Potter grumbled from the corner.

Murphy glared at him, then turned back to me. "So you think those red waters made you well – cured you in some way?"

"The dead waters," I whispered. Then looking at Murphy, I added, "It's the only difference between what happened to me and your daughters."

"Sam called them the Dead Waters," Murphy said. "Sam said that the waters will heal us. If we bathe in them, they will stop us from turning to stone."

"So they do have healing properties," I breathed.

"And so does *Olay Essentials*, or so they say," Potter cut in. "But you don't see me prancing about wearing it."

Ignoring him, I looked at Murphy and said, "This could be part of the answer we've been looking for."

I couldn't help but think of what the Elders had said to me in the graveyard. They had told me that if I didn't choose between the Vampyrus and the humans, then my friends and I would turn to stone in this *pushed* world and be trapped here forever like statues. But what if the dead waters stopped us from turning to stone? Then that would mean there was a flaw in the Elders' plan. Perhaps there were more flaws that they hadn't seen or perhaps weren't telling me about? Perhaps I could go back with my friends if I *pushed* everything back? And there was someone else. Someone Jack had told me to go and find...someone who knew about the whole *push* thing...someone who was called...

"What are you thinking about?" Murphy cut in.

"Huh?" I said.

"You looked lost in thought," he said.

"It was nothing." I shook my head as if waking from a deep sleep.

Another silence fell over the room as if we were all lost to our own private thoughts. My mind raced with everything I had learnt since coming to this house – to this room. The Elders had been right about one thing. They had said that by choosing to seek out my father in this world, I had started along a path which would lead me to the person who would ultimately make me choose between the humans and the Vampyrus.

My train of thought was disturbed by the sound of a chair scrapping backwards across the rough wooden floorboards. I glanced up to see Murphy standing. He then hunkered down, and lifted his brother's body into his arms.

"What are you doing?" I asked him.

"I'm going to bury him," he said. "Do you want to come? He was your father."

"No," I said softly. "I buried my father in the world before it got *pushed*. I don't think I can do it again."

"Fair enough," Murphy said, heading towards the door, carrying his brother. "Get some rest while I'm gone. When I get back, we'll set off in search of Kayla and Sam, then head for the Dead Waters."

Then he was gone, the sound of his heavy footfalls disappearing down the stairs.

Chapter Thirty

Kiera

Without having to look up, I knew Potter was staring at me. Murphy might have explained his reason for lying to me and keeping the truth from me all these years, but Potter was still yet to offer up his excuses. To be honest, I didn't know if I was ready to hear them. However much I tried, I couldn't get those images of him with that teacher out of my head. To know that he had also lied to me about his relationship with Eloisa also hurt. And although I pretended I didn't care, I did wonder what he thought of me, now that he knew what I really was and where I had come from. Would any of that knowledge change his feelings towards me?

With his staring eyes making me feel uncomfortable, I stood up and looked out of the window. The first weak rays of winter sunlight were shining over the horizon. I looked down and could see Murphy slowly making his way through the snow, down the hill towards the graveyard. He looked a solitary figure, and although part of me still felt anger at what he had kept from me, there was another part of me which understood his reasons. All of the decisions he had made - right or wrong – Murphy had been trying to protect the people he loved most: Pen, his brother and my father, his daughters, and I knew in my heart he had been trying to protect me, too.

I felt a hand fall on my shoulder. I knew it was Potter who had crept up behind me. I shrugged his hand away.

"I'm sorry," he whispered.

"Yeah, and so am I," I whispered back. "I'm sorry I gave you my heart to rip in half."

We stood quietly and watched Murphy disappear from

view, his dead brother draped over his arms. In the distance there was something else, just faint like a charcoal smudge.

"More statues," Potter said thoughtfully.

"Yes," I nodded, glancing down at the faint cracks which had started to appear across the back of my hands again.

Another uncomfortable silence, as if neither of us knew what to say.

"Do you think Murphy will ever see Pen – Lilly Blu – or whatever her name is, again?" Potter suddenly asked me.

"Yes," I said, looking out of the window.

"How can you be so sure?"

Without looking at him, I said, "Jack, told me I had to find her."

'Dead Water'

(Kiera Hudson Series Two)
Book 7
Now Available

More books by Tim O'Rourke

Kiera Hudson Series One
Vampire Shift (Kiera Hudson Series 1) Book 1
Vampire Wake (Kiera Hudson Series 1) Book 2
Vampire Hunt (Kiera Hudson Series 1) Book 3
Vampire Breed (Kiera Hudson Series 1) Book 4
Wolf House (Kiera Hudson Series 1) Book 5
Vampire Hollows (Kiera Hudson Series 1) Book 6
Kiera Hudson Series Two
Dead Flesh (Kiera Hudson Series 2) Book 1
Dead Night (Kiera Hudson Series 2) Book 2
Dead Angels (Kiera Hudson Series 2) Book 3
Dead Statues (Kiera Hudson Series 2) Book 4
Dead Seth (Kiera Hudson Series 2) Book 5
Dead Wolf (Kiera Hudson Series 2) Book 6
Dead Water (Kiera Hudson Series 2) Book 7
Dead Push (Kiera Hudson Series 2) Book 8
Dead Lost (Kiera Hudson Series 2) Book 9
Dead End (Kiera Hudson Series 2) Book 10
Kiera Hudson Series Three
The Creeping Men (Kiera Hudson Series Three) Book 1
The Lethal Infected (Kiera Hudson Series Three) Book 2
The Adoring Artist (Kiera Hudson Series Three) Book 3
The Secret Identity (Kiera Hudson Series Three) Book 4
The White Wolf (Kiera Hudson Series Three) Book 5

The Origins of Cara (Kiera Hudson Series Three) Book 6
The Final Push (Kiera Hudson Series Three) Book 7
The Underground Switch (Kiera Hudson Series Three) Book 8
The Last Elder (Kiera Hudson Series Three) Book 9
Kiera Hudson Series Four
The Girl Who Travelled Backward (Book 1)
The Man Who Loved Sone (Book 2)
Kiera Hudson & the Six Clicks
The Six Clicks (Book 1)
The Kiera Hudson Prequels
The Kiera Hudson Prequels (Book One)
The Kiera Hudson Prequels (Book Two)
Kiera Hudson & Sammy Carter
Vampire Twin (*Pushed* Trilogy) Book 1
Vampire Chronicle (*Pushed* Trilogy) Book 2
The Alternate World of Kiera Hudson
Wolf Shift (Book One)
After Dark (Book Two)
The Beautiful Immortals
The Beautiful Immortals (Book One)
The Beautiful Immortals (Book Two)
The Beautiful Immortals (Book Three)
The Beautiful Immortals (Book Four)
The Beautiful Immortals (Book Five)
The Beautiful Immortals (Book Six)
The Laura Pepper Trilogy
Vampires of Fogmin Moor (Book One)
Vampires of Fogmin Moor (Book Two)
Vampires of Fogmin Moor (Book Three)
The Mirror Realm (The Lacey Swift Series)
The Mirror Realm (Book One)
The Mirror Realm (Book Two)
The Mirror Realm (Book Three)

The Mirror Realm (Book Four)

Moon Trilogy

Moonlight (Moon Trilogy) Book 1

Moonbeam (Moon Trilogy) Book 2

Moonshine (Moon Trilogy) Book 3

The Clockwork Immortals

Stranger (Part One)

Stranger (Part Two)

Stranger (Part Three)

The Jack Seth Novellas

Hollow Pit (Book One)

Black Hill Farm (Books 1 & 2)

Black Hill Farm (Book 1)

Black Hill Farm: Andy's Diary (Book 2)

Sidney Hart Novels

Witch (A Sidney Hart Novel) Book 1

Yellow (A Sidney Hart Novel) Book 2

The Tessa Dark Trilogy

Stilts (Book 1)

Zip (Book 2)

The Mechanic

The Mechanic

The Dark Side of Nightfall Trilogy

The Dark Side of Nightfall (Book One)

The Dark Side of Nightfall (Book Two)

The Dark Side of Nightfall (Book Three)

Samantha Carter Series

Vampire Seeker (Book One)

Vampire Flappers (Book Two)

Vampire Watchmen (Book Three)

The Charley Shepard Series

Saving the Dead (Book One)

Unscathed

Written by Tim O'Rourke & C.J. Pinard
You can contact Tim O'Rourke at
www.facebook.com/timorourkeauthor/ or by email at
kierahudson91@aol.com

Printed in Great Britain
by Amazon

10455345R00109